November
Storm

The

Iowa

Short

Fiction

Award

In honor of

James O. Freedman

University

of Iowa Press

Iowa City

*Robert
Oldshue*

*November
Storm*

Oldshue

University of Iowa Press, Iowa City 52242

Copyright © 2016 by Robert Oldshue

www.uiowapress.org

Printed in the United States of America

The University of Iowa Press is a member of Green Press
Initiative and is committed to preserving natural resources.
Printed on acid-free paper

Library of Congress Cataloging-in-Publication Data

Names: Oldshue, Robert, author.

Title: November storm / Robert Oldshue.

Description: Iowa City : University Of Iowa Press, 2016. |
Series: Iowa Short Fiction Award

Identifiers: LCCN 2016007493 | ISBN 978-1-60938-451-7 (pbk) |
ISBN 978-1-60938-452-4 (ebk)

Subjects: LCSH: Life change events—Fiction. | Change
(Psychology)—Fiction. | Psychological fiction. | BISAC:
FICTION / Short Stories (single author).

Classification: LCC PS3615.L423 A6 2016 | DDC 813/.6—dc23

LC record available at https://lccn.loc.gov/2016007493

For Nina. Always.

Contents

ACKNOWLEDGMENTS

I would like to thank my teachers Andre Dubus III, Pablo Medina, A. Manette Ansay, C. J. Hribal, David Haynes, Susan Neville, Peter Turchi, and Kevin McIlvoy. I would also like to thank my classmate at Warren Wilson, Shannon Cain, who edited this collection and told me to believe in it. I would also like to thank, for their friendship and support, Warren Wilson alums Tracy Winn and Helen Fremont, novelist Rosamund Lupton and her husband Martin Lupton, M.D., as well as Amanda Lebus, Gail Levine, and my ever patient family, my wife, Nina, and my children, Kate and Sam.

These stories appeared originally in the following journals: "November Storm," "The Receiving Line," and "The Field of Machpelah" in *New England Review*; "Home Depot" and "The Home of the Holy Assumption" (the latter as "The Mona Lisa") in the *Bellevue Literary Review*; and "Mass Mental" and "Summer Friend" in the *Gettysburg Review*.

November
Storm

November
Storm

That Thanksgiving, Andy was coming, so Doris thought the call was from him. "Maybe he's got car trouble," she said when the phone rang.

"Maybe he's got someplace better to go," said her husband, Ed.

But it was a woman from Wegmans, the grocery that had their dinner. "Because of the snow, we're canceling deliveries."

"It isn't snowing here," Doris told her.

"A foot by noon and two feet by tonight and wind chills of thirty below."

"They said a dusting or maybe nothing."

"That's not what they're saying now, ma'am. I'm sorry, ma'am."

It was shortly before nine, and, if Andy hadn't called, he and Jen and the grandchildren were out on I-90, facing the kind of storms there could be in upstate New York. When the boys were still swimming, the family had driven to a meet in Corning, in the winter, and the weather had gotten bad and then worse and there'd been talk of stopping the meet early. Some of the parents had taken their boys and gone home, but Dan had done well in his qualifying heats, and Tom was on a relay that would lose if he didn't stay, and Andy was too young to participate but was generally willing to sit and watch. By the time it was over, the snow was coming in sheets and there was wind, and, by the time they hit the Thruway, the road was a mess but Ed was beyond talking to. If we stop, no telling when we can start again, he kept saying. No telling how much work I'll have to miss and how much school for the boys and, even if we find a motel, how are we going to eat for two days? Now he was somebody's eighty-year-old grandpa stooped and swaying in her kitchen, his once handsome face puffy, his hair white and wild, his hands dusky and sometimes shaking, the backs covered with ragged, red spots.

"Well?" she asked when she'd given him the news.

"Well, what?"

"Well, what do you think?"

"What am I supposed to think?"

Doris thought how easily she or anyone could send him sprawling with a push. Instead she asked if they could get the dinner themselves, and the woman said they could.

"Could someone help us load it in the car?"

"Absolutely," said the woman.

"And you'll have it all ready?"

"I'll put it together now."

Doris told her they'd be over and hung up, and Ed waved his hands as if, after fifty-three years of marriage, he'd finally seen everything.

"Why'd you let them get away with it?"

"It isn't them. It's the storm."

"What storm?" he roared, pointing to the window and through it to their street, Royal Crescent. A snowflake drifted past, another, several. For a moment there were none, and then there were another two or three, and, by the time Ed had tried the weather channel and heard about a flood in Texas and Doris had tried Andy's cell and gotten a series of recordings, the flakes were more than just a few.

"What's that?" Doris asked when Ed had backed the car out and she'd gotten in, their places on the front seat separated by an old rubber boot.

"I want to get the buckle fixed," he said.

"Does it have to be today?"

"Yeah," he growled. "If it's going to snow."

The house across the street had been the Spectors', and, in the 1950s, when the houses had been built, Helen Spector had invited Doris and the other Royal mothers for coffee, and they'd sat in her kitchen and talked about their children and their husbands and their houses and the schools and what they'd seen on television or at the movies. As the kids had gotten older, the coffees had gotten fewer and then stopped, and then Dick Spector had passed, and Helen had sold the house to a couple with a motorboat who'd sold it to a man who lived alone and kept his shades drawn and the car in the garage with the door closed, and now it was owned by a woman with an eleven-year-old son and a boyfriend Doris sometimes saw and sometimes didn't. The next house was the Bromleys', Pete and Betty, whose son had weight-lifted with Dan and Tom when the two of them were doing it twice a day and drinking carrot juice and other concoctions that were fine with Doris as long as they paid for them and said what was in them and didn't leave them rotting in the refrigerator. They'd had a daughter a year behind Dan who'd been a cheerleader when Dan was playing football, but by then Betty was unhappy with the house, and they'd bought a bigger one a mile or so away, and, except once in a while around town, Doris never saw them again. In fact, of all the first families, there were just them and the Olneys, and the Olneys had a cottage in Maine they went to every summer, and Doris and Ed had a condo in Florida they went to every winter, and, besides, Ed had gone to college but a technical institute not a liberal arts college, and Doris had finished high school but that was all. The Olneys had met at Oberlin, and Sue had studied painting and sculpture and still took lessons and filled their house with pieces she'd done and others she'd collected and went to museum shows and lectures and films and read books and thought about them, and Paul was a chemist and worked at Kodak, the same as Ed, but the two of them might have been from different planets. They might have fought for different countries in the war, or so it seemed when the discussion came to politics, which, thanks to the women, it never did. Rather than watch Paul stiffen as Ed supported Reagan or even Nixon or mocked the do-gooding lame brains opposed to nuclear energy, everyone spoke in coded generalities until Ed began to fidget and then nod and Doris had to wake him up and take everybody home. Once the kids were gone, the two couples had settled into watching each other's comings and goings and promising, when they met, to get together soon.

"Looks like the Olneys are away," Doris said as they passed.

"What?"

"Paul and Sue. They usually have Thanksgiving with the Teetermans but the house is all dark and I haven't seen them today."

"Are the Teetermans people I'm supposed to know?"

"Don and Loretta."

"Never heard of them."

"They have a son named Jeff and a daughter named Tracy. Jeff was a year ahead of Dan, and Tracy was a year ahead of Tom, and Don and Loretta were in Parent's Forum."

"Everybody was in Parent's Forum."

After Royal, they turned onto Pine Crest and drove past the Sullivans' house, or former house. The Sullivans were an older couple; their children were grown by the time Doris and Ed had their three. Doris only knew they were the Sullivans because it said so on the wrought iron lamppost in their yard, and she'd only known that Mr. Sullivan had gone to a nursing home when she no longer saw him in the yard and that's what someone had said. After that the yard had been cut by someone Doris never saw until one day the sign was gone and there was a car she didn't know in the driveway, and, after that, when she drove by, Doris looked at the house and looked away, as she did now but only after she'd noticed the yard and the driveway and the roof, noting that there wasn't any snow on the roof or on the roof of the next house, formerly the Weinbergers', or the next house, formerly the Ginns'. Then they turned onto Indian Trail and the houses were bigger and older and there were fewer that she knew or had ever known, just the Isaacs' where there was nothing on the yard or driveway and what little was on the roof she couldn't see for sure. There might have been the faintest whitening, or it might have been the uncertain black-gray color of the roof; she'd never before had reason to look at it closely or the roof on the next house, a house that had once caught fire. Again the yard and the driveway were fine, and the road was still fine, but the roof looked a little whiter than she remembered or a little softer, or maybe a roof wasn't something you could remember exactly. Then they turned onto List and passed the grade school, and there was no longer any doubt. Just beyond it was the middle school, and, just beyond that, was the high school, and the snow gusted in great, dark swarms across the fields that ran between and all around the schools. It seemed to consume them and with them her boys, her memory of her boys, her memory of all the years they'd gone to one or the other of the schools and she'd dropped them off and picked them up and gone to conferences with their teachers and concerts and plays and P.T.A. and Parent's Forum meetings and swim meets and baseball and football and lacrosse games. She felt as if the storm was ready to consume a part of her, and she was relieved when they were past the schools and entered the commercial strip that separated Irondequoit, their town, from the city.

A sign in the shoemaker's window said, Closed.

"He's closed," said Doris when they pulled in.

"How do you know?"

"The sign."

"What sign?"

Doris pointed, and Ed looked, but he turned off the motor and got out.

"What are you doing?"

"I want to see for myself."

"See what for yourself?"

"If he's there."

"How could he be there?"

"How should I know? People do all kinds of crazy things."

He walked up along the car, one hand on the hood, one hand holding the boot as he took his now slow and careful steps to the door and looked in, and Doris wondered how long the sign had been there. She wondered how the shoemaker could still be in business. He'd been there since she remembered, and he'd never

seemed old, but he'd never seemed young, and, anyway, everybody they knew had gotten old. Maybe he had a son who was
helping him or a nephew or some other kind of help, or maybe he
was old but, by some miracle, hanging on, or maybe he'd sold the
business and she hadn't heard. After walking to the window and
looking through it and looking, again, at the sign and then, again,
through the window, Ed walked back along the car and got in.

"He's closed," he said, brushing the snow off his pants.

Until the sixties, it was just another supermarket in a plaza
further down Hudson. Doris had taken the boys when they were
little and let them go on increasingly long searches for what she
needed, and, whenever they got bored, she could go on about her
shopping and know that people would be watching and that she'd
hear if the boys called. Over the years, she got to know where
everything was on every shelf, and she got to know Bob in the
meat department and Ted in the bakery and Delores and Vivian
at check-out and all the people she didn't know except by sight but
always nodded to and sometimes spoke to, and, sometimes, there
was one or another of the Wegmans themselves. Then they'd built
the first of the new superstores, a monstrosity the size of a commercial jet hangar or convention hall, and Doris occasionally saw
people from Royal or the surrounding streets or some other parent from one or another of the boys' schools or sports teams but it
was never as comfortable. The conversation always drifted toward
the size of the place, the challenge of finding things or finding
your shopping cart if you left it on one of the thirty-odd aisles,
and, while prices were good and the selection was amazing and
the employees were courteous and competent and attractive and
professionally dressed, you never saw them twice or seemed to
and their friendliness was the kind that left you feeling as if you
didn't have a friend in the world. With the holiday and the storm,
the parking lot was jammed, and, inside, because the holiday had
left the store short of staff, things were even worse. Despite her
efforts to pull him one way or the other, Ed kept running into
people, and, when they got to the deli section, the counter was

three and four deep, and there was just the one woman doing everything.

"Can I help you?" she asked when it was finally their turn. But when Ed said their name, she stopped, as if startled.

"What's the matter?"

"Your dinner."

"What's wrong with it now?"

"Nothing, but—I didn't know. I mean, I couldn't tell on the phone."

"You couldn't tell *what* on the phone? We've seen bigger storms than this. We drove all the way to Corning in a storm like this. Remember that, Dory? Remember that swim meet? We didn't let it bother us. We just jumped in the car and barreled through."

"Boom!" he said, making a fist and thrusting it at the woman.

But when the woman had gotten their dinner and put it in a box and gotten a boy to carry it, the snow had changed from flakes to a steady, bone-white powder, and seeing it through the window by the exit, Ed wanted candles, batteries too. "Meet you at the car," he said and stomped off, leaving Doris to realize that she didn't have a key.

"You don't have to wait," she told the boy.

"I'm fine."

"We could come get you."

"I'm fine. Really."

The boy's hair was moussed into short, yellow spikes, and one of his ears was pierced with a ring, and there was stubble on his jaw that spread disreputably up his otherwise smooth and youthful cheeks. For all the anger of his appearance, someone had taught him to be polite to old people, so Doris continued. "Have you worked here long?"

"Since the summer."

"When do you do your schoolwork?"

She asked where he went to school and expected him to say Irondequoit, the high school her boys had attended. Instead, he said East Ridge, the school across town.

"Will Thanksgiving be at home?"

"We're going to my aunt's house."

"Will she be cooking?"

"She's cooking some, and my mom's cooking some and bringing it over, and my other aunt and my uncle and my grandmother are cooking."

"So everybody's helping. That's nice."

Doris spoke as if she'd had many such Thanksgivings, although they'd had only one. She and Ed were from Chicago, and, when the boys were old enough, they'd driven there for the holiday but had found the traffic impossible and hadn't done it again.

"How many will you be?"

Twenty-eight, twenty-nine with his brother's new baby, the boy replied, and Doris wondered if she and Ed had made a mistake. At every opportunity, they'd prepared their boys to leave home and they had. She'd helped them with their grade school and middle school homework, and Ed had helped them, in high school, with their chemistry, physics, and calculus. He'd encouraged them to be practical and self-reliant, and Dan had gone to Carnegie Mellon and had studied computer science and worked for an investment bank in New York, and Tom had gone to Cornell and had studied hotel management and worked for a chain in California, and Andy had gotten lost at Ohio State but had found himself and gone to social work school and worked with the probate department in Cleveland and had a wife who was a speech pathologist. West Irondequoit had all the scientists from Kodak, the main industry in Rochester, and East Irondequoit had everybody else, and, with lower incomes to tax, the east had lower budgets, lower salaries, less equipment, and fewer teams that won and fewer kids that went to college. But maybe they'd been lucky, Doris thought as the boy said that his aunt was cooking three twenty-five-pound turkeys.

"Could I ask you a personal question?"

The boy smiled the way her boys had smiled when, by some irreproducible accident, she or someone else had gotten beneath their need to act like Ed. "That depends."

"Could I ask about your earring?"

"What about it?"

"Did it hurt?"

"A little."

"Does it hurt now?"

"No."

"Not when you catch it on things? That's why I never got one."

"That's why I got a small one."

"It is elegant," Doris admitted. "Do people like it?"

"Some people."

"Your mom?"

"Yeah."

"But not your dad."

"No."

"Why not?"

"He thinks it means I'm queer."

"What does it mean?"

"It means I have an earring," the boy replied with an emphasis he'd used while fighting with his dad, Doris was sure.

"I think he'll get over it."

"I don't know."

"I do. I think he respects you."

The boy shifted the weight of the box in his arms. "Then why did he make me walk?"

"Walk where?"

"To the piercing place. He wouldn't give me a ride, and he wouldn't let my mom give me a ride, and he wouldn't let her pay."

Doris was about to reply when Ed returned and took her by the arm and the three of them went outside where the snow stung Doris' face and bare hands so badly that she closed her eyes and nearly fell. The footing was unsure, and Doris pulled on Ed, and Ed pulled on Doris until the boy took the dinner in one arm and used his other to guide them to the car where he helped them get in, after which Doris told the boy goodbye and good luck and felt relaxed for the first time since the woman had called that morning. In a minute, they'd be home and could put the dinner in the oven and light a fire in the living room fireplace and set out some cheese and crackers and olives and nuts, and, once Andy arrived, the snow wouldn't matter. They could watch it come down and feel safe and happy with the fire and each other and the dinner they'd earned whether or not they'd done the cooking.

But when Ed started the car and drove from the parking lot back onto Hudson, he failed to see a car coming from his right and struck it, their big Cadillac crushing Sue Olney's little Honda so badly that she could no longer drive.

"Who's that?"

"I don't know."

"Then why's she waving at us?"

Doris again said she didn't know, but then, very slowly, her nerves still singing, her thinking still startled and slightly foreign, she recognized the Honda, a blue one, the sticker from the art gallery on the back left window and the familiar face grinning from the front left window.

"That's Sue."

"Sue who?" asked Ed.

"Our neighbor, Sue—Sue Olney."

"What's *she* doing here?"

After checking that Doris was O.K. and assuring her that he was, he pulled the car around, up in front of Sue's car and parked it against the curb and opened his door just long enough for snow to blow in, all over them. Cars were honking and pulling around and backed up in both directions, but Ed looked at the boot and put it on and got out, and—watching his upper body swing and pivot— Doris could tell what he was doing. He was putting his weight to the left, booted foot, using it for traction as he took smaller, lighter steps with his right until he got to Doris and used his left foot to clear a place for her and opened her door and helped her out. By then Sue had gotten out, and they joined her on the curb, only Ed with a hat, only Sue wearing gloves, their heads and shoulders frosted by the thickly falling grains.

"I thought it was you," Sue said, laughing. "How nice to run into you."

"I'm so sorry," said Doris.

"Forget it. Besides, we haven't talked in months. How are you? How was your summer? Say, Ed, you're missing a boot."

"It's a long story."

"Life's a long story," Sue continued, waving her hand as if to wave the weather away. "We're supposed to be having dinner with the Teetermans but Paul got chest pain in the middle of the night and they've got him up at North Side."

"No!" said Doris.

"Oh, he's fine. And his tests are all fine but you know how hospitals are. They keep telling me, 'At his age you can't take any chances.' As if I wouldn't know. I was just running home to get him a change of clothes and something to read and to shower and change clothes myself before the storm hit."

"Looks like it hit," said Ed.

"And then some," she replied, laughing, and Doris wondered why she was acting the way she was. Her husband was sick, and she'd just missed being hurt or even killed herself, and now she was stuck in a blizzard with a car she'd have to have towed, and she was talking as if she were chatting beside a pool.

Had she hit her head? Was she in a state of shock?

"Speaking of Wegmans, you'll never guess who I saw the other day, Doris. Remember Mr. Brewster?"

"No, I'm afraid I don't."

"Oh, sure you do. The band teacher."

"At the high school?"

"At the middle school."

"Arnie Brewster!" Ed exclaimed. "There's a guy I haven't thought about in twenty years."

"Longer," said Doris.

"I wish it were twenty years," said Sue. "Anyway, I saw this man in one of the first aisles, and he looked familiar but I couldn't place him, and I was trying not to stare, but he looked so familiar, it was driving me crazy. And you know how it is at a grocery store, you run into somebody on the first aisle, and you see them on the next aisle and the next. I was running into him for the third or fourth time and wondering who he was but trying not to stare when he stopped and looked at me and said, 'You had a son named Todd who played the flute and a son named A. J. who played the trombone and a daughter named Lauren who played the clarinet.'"

"How on earth did he remember?" asked Doris.

"He said he's been retired for fifteen years but still remembers all the kids," said Sue. "He said he had a daughter in the high school when A. J. was there, which means she was there when Dan and Tom were there. Did you know that? Do you remember a girl named Brewster?"

"What was her first name?"

"Anne, I think he said. Anne or maybe Diane."

A man stopped and pulled his S.U.V. up, over the curb, alongside their cars but out of danger of being hit. He told them to get in and get warm, and Ed told the ladies to go ahead, he'd stay out and wait for the police, which he did until an officer came and looked at the cars and at Ed and his one boot and then looked at the S.U.V.

"You ladies see the accident?"

"Are you kidding, officer? We *are* the accident!" Sue replied so gaily he looked at her as he'd just looked at Ed. He asked if anyone was hurt, and Sue said no, they were fine, so he called a tow truck but not an ambulance, and, a few minutes later, the truck roared away with Sue's car and the three of them continued home in the Cadillac, which had damage to the bumper and the grill but was drivable.

"Not here yet," said Doris when they got to the Olneys'. She was looking three driveways down to their own.

"They'll get here," Ed replied.

"They're probably wondering where you are," said Sue. "They've probably been calling and calling, so I'd better let you go."

Doris and Ed were sitting in the front, and Sue was sitting in the back, and they'd already said they'd help her with her car, fixing it and paying for anything the insurance didn't cover and getting her to the hospital to see Paul or anywhere else she needed. They said it all again, but she insisted that she was fine, she could drive Paul's car, a Subaru, a four-wheel drive, or she could call and ask the Teetermans. She thanked them for the lift and told them not to feel bad and started to get out but saw the flagstone walk, now just a line of oblong depressions leading from the driveway to their door in the front.

"You want me to shovel it?" Ed asked.

"Oh, it's not that," she replied. "I was thinking about the day Paul made it."

"I remember that day," said Doris.

"You do?"

"Yes. I looked out the kitchen window and saw your old Chevy station wagon all down to the ground with something heavy and Paul pulling out flagstones and trying not to drop them on—Todd, I guess it was. You only had the one child, I remember."

"Do you remember how hot it was?" Sue asked. "Do you remember how hot it always was back then? There weren't any trees so there wasn't any shade. We just had the ash in the front and the locust and the ornamental cherry in the back, all of them saplings."

"And we just had our maple and the little willow," said Doris. "We could see from our house to the Greens' house at the other end."

"And they could see us," said Ed. "We had to keep our shades down."

"Oh, Ed," said Doris.

"But he's right," said Sue. "There weren't any trees, and all the houses were right next to each other and all at ground level, and, with all the kids, you never knew what they'd left open or closed or which ten of them would walk in when. Do you know that there were sixty children on Royal between the ages of five and fifteen? Mary Cuthpert and Phyllis Rush and I sat at the block party the year the Bergethons had it and that's what we came up with. Sixty-two. Now there might be a dozen, and you never see them out playing, not together, not like they used to. They're all different ages now."

"They're all in day care now," said Ed. "They're all from different families. You talk to a neighbor now and they tell you this kid's from that father and this one's from that mother and the kid's with the father this week and the mother that week and some other father the next week. Now there's all kinds of people living on the street."

"And there's us," said Sue. "What kind of people are we?"

Doris was turned sideways in her seat and looking back as they talked, so she noticed when Sue began to tremble. She didn't know if she was laughing or crying or finally reacting to what had happened or whether she was simply cold.

"Paul took his shirt off," Sue continued, still trembling although her speech was steady. "That day with the flagstones, he took it off, and I didn't care, but I didn't know if the neighbors would, so I asked him to put it back on. We used to think about things like that. We used to think about a lot of things nobody thinks about now."

For a moment, no one spoke, and there was just the throb of the motor and the steady flop-flop of the wipers and the silent fall of the snow on the windshield, on the hood, and on the windows all around them. Then Doris asked about the hospital again.

"If you don't want us to drive, we understand, but Andy should be here soon and he could drive you, and I know he wouldn't mind."

Sue looked at her. The trembling stopped.

"When was the last time you saw Andy?"

"August."

"And how many days will he be here—two, maybe three?"

Sue reached over the seat and gently squeezed Doris on the upper arm, and Doris realized that in all their years of watching and knowing everything about each other's lives they'd never hugged or even shaken hands. They'd never been close enough to make it comfortable or distant enough to make it casual, and, anyway, with neighbors there was never any rush. They were always going to be there.

"Have a nice holiday," Sue said.

"Thank you," Doris replied, putting her free hand on top of Sue's and looking directly at her. "Have a nice holiday."

"Yeah," said Ed. "And say the same to Paul."

"I will," said Sue.

She got from the car and ignored the ankle-deep snow on the walk until she reached the step which was clear enough that she could stamp the snow from her feet and bend and brush her ankles and the bottom of her slacks before she opened the door and went inside and switched on a lamp as it was by then afternoon and the light was already weakening. She waved from a window, and they both waved back, and Ed eased the car down the driveway and then down the street to their own driveway, pulling slightly past it before slowly backing in.

"What are you doing now?"

"I don't know about the engine. It might not start again."

He said that if they had to call for a tow, the car should face out so the tow truck could hook it up. He pushed the button for the door and tried to back in the narrow, single-car garage. But the driveway was slick, and the wheels kept spinning, and the car kept sliding, and, after two attempts, he stopped and left it, and, when Andy arrived, he asked what it was doing there and was upset when they explained. He asked if they'd been hurt. He asked if Sue had been hurt. He asked if Ed had gotten a ticket, and instead of the celebration Doris had imagined, instead of talking to Sadie about her first year at school and to Ben about the ray gun he was aiming at everybody and asking more about the drive from Cleveland and how awful it must have been and how grateful she and Ed were that they'd come anyway, Doris kept asking herself the question Andy kept stepping around: when would they be too old to drive and how they would know and what would any of them do then? What if Paul died or was too sick to live at home again and Sue moved away and she and Ed were the last ones on Royal, the last of all those young families who'd helped each other and owed each other?

And to make things worse, instead of showing any worry or any respect for Andy's worry, Ed kept dismissing him, needling him the way he needled all the boys but, for some reason, needled Andy in particular.

"Your mother's talking like it was a major collision."

"Wasn't it? I thought Mrs. Olney got her car wrecked."

"It wasn't wrecked."

"Could she drive it?"

"She didn't try. The police didn't let her try. And anyway, she's got a Honda, so who cares? Those cars don't have a chassis. All they are is folded-over sheet metal. They're wrecked if you tap 'em with your finger."

"You could have killed her, Dad."

"Don't blame me. Blame the Japanese. Blame her for buying the damn car."

Then, when dinner was ready, Ed was missing and Doris let herself feel the anger she'd been controlling all day.

If only she'd left him at home!

If only she'd gone to get the dinner herself! If only she hadn't married him!

Her first year in high school, she'd passed the gym and heard shouting and looked in and seen a lot of boys and one boy sitting on the floor, against the wall, watching the other boys play basketball. He was wearing shorts and a T-shirt, and she remembered the length of his legs and the power in his arms and the ease and power of his attention. But mostly it was the profile she'd noticed, the set of his head, a small but particular angle that made it look as if whatever problem he looked at long enough he could solve. It was back in the Depression, and, of all the boys at Peltner High, he'd looked like the one who'd make it, and he had. And as much as he'd changed, as much as his posture had stooped and his once graceful movements had stiffened and failed, he could still look at things and get that angle, that power, and the years would, for an instant, disappear. It had happened that morning when he'd tried to get the weather report. He'd turned on the television but hadn't got a picture, just a blank, blue screen, and had fiddled with the cable box, his attention youthful and complete. It had happened that afternoon, when he and Andy had argued. She'd bought the grandchildren gifts and given Ben a model airplane, and he brought it to Ed to put together, and despite the distraction, despite the fact that she sat there wishing he'd brought Andy or even her the plane, there it was, that focus, that confidence.

And, now, there it was again.

After looking around the house, she'd gone to the kitchen and looked out the window and seen the great, white flakes the snow had changed back to. The woman in the Spectors' old house had a light on her porch, and they had one on theirs, so the flakes were lit from the front and from behind and very pretty, and Doris stood and watched them tumbling and shining until she saw one place where the darkness seemed darker than it should or the snow seemed less or maybe her eyes were playing tricks on her. No there it was; there *he* was. She wasn't sure until she saw his head, that angle of his head. He was standing at the end of the driveway. He was wearing no coat, but he was wearing his boots, both of them; she looked until she could just see the tops above the deepening drifts. For a moment, she thought they'd had it, that the accident or hearing about Paul or the stress of the grandchildren visiting or arguing with Andy had driven him over the edge, that he'd wandered out crazed, until she saw what he was looking at—the car, the Cadillac, the kind of car two poor kids from south Chicago could never hope to own. He was out there inspecting it, wondering, she supposed, the cost of fixing it, and, furious, she went to the front door and threw it open ready to shout his name.

But the wind had died, and the air was cold and would carry what she said, and the houses would bounce it up and down the street as if a dozen fed-up housewives were shouting. She looked over at the Olneys' and saw that, like many of the houses, it was dark and that snow had covered the roof and the driveway and the yard so smoothly, so perfectly, it appeared that Sue and Paul were gone, which before long they would be. Before long some other family would come and make the house theirs; and then another and another, and the Olneys would be forgotten, just as the others had, just as her parents had, just as she and Ed would be forgotten.

"How's it look?" she asked.

"Not bad," he said, as he pulled on a piece of trim. "But I'll have to look in the daylight. I'll have to open up the hood and look inside. How's dinner?"

"It's ready."

"Is everybody sitting down?"

"Yes."

"Why didn't you say something?"

"I am," she replied, feeling her anger rise again but this time feeling it rise through and past her and up into the night and the cold and what was left of the storm. It was like speaking a new language or one she'd forgotten. It was like standing in that other door, the one at the gym, wondering what to do, what to say when that long-armed boy suddenly turned his head and looked at her.

"I'm sorry, Ed."

"Oh, that's O.K. I didn't tell you I was out here."

"I mean, I'm sorry about the accident."

"What about it?"

"I'm sorry I didn't see it coming."

"You weren't driving."

"I could have looked. I could have looked out my side and told you what I saw."

Ed stood before her, a stranger, a ghost floating in some cold and shining nowhere she had once called her life.

But she knew what he would say.

What he always said. Come on, Dory! As in, Come on, Dory, you're being silly! Or, Come on, Dory, you'll make us late!

"Come on, Dory!" he said now. "We made it, didn't we? Who cares about the rest?"

The
Receiving
Line

It was 1978, and I was gay, and I was poor, and, when necessary, I made a little money from sex. I lived in Boston, not far from the Common, and I'd go there and sit on a bench and watch for men who were watching for me.

"Nice day," they'd say.

"Nice day," I'd reply until the men like the days all seemed to be the same.

I went with a cop and a dentist and a telephone repairman. I went with a baggage handler at Logan Airport who turned out to be a friend of my brother's. I went with a state senator. I went with him a few times. We did it in his office at the state house, which is next to the Common. I'd pretend to be a messenger. He'd pretend to be annoyed.

"You're late!" he'd say if our meeting was on.

And then there was Anthony. "Nice day." He stopped in front of me and looked so uncomfortable, I said it to him.

"What?" he asked.

"Nice day. Nice weather."

"It's freezing," he snapped, looking around as if at an audience who agreed.

"Good thing you've got a hat."

It was February, and he was wearing a fur hat with flaps and aviator sunglasses. He was trying to be discrete but only drew more attention. And when he asked what I charged, he whispered and then shouted.

"That's a rip-off!" he complained so loudly that I left, afraid of arrest, only to find, when I looked, that he was following me.

Every time I stopped, he stopped, and every time I started, he started, so we stopped and started all the way to the hotel at which point he disappeared.

"That's the last I'll see of him," I thought as I returned to my bench.

But the next afternoon, as I left my day job, he was waiting across the street. He stared at me and, for a short distance, followed me. And that night, I saw him at my night job. I worked days cutting hair and worked nights tending bar, and he walked into the bar and looked around and walked out again. And then he came to my apartment.

"I have to confront him," I said, interrupting Sunday brunch.

"Confront who?" asked Benny.

"Whom?" Tim corrected.

"The guy with the hat."

"What guy with what hat?"

"*Which* guy with *which* hat?" Dave corrected Tim, interested only until I told him. "That's prostitution," he said.

"There are worse things."

"Like what?"

Like marrying your high school sweetheart only to discover, three years and two children later, that Mr. Hanratty's sex education class covered everybody's sex but yours. Like hiring a divorce lawyer only to discover that he hates you as does the judge who sets alimony so high you can't go to school, you can't buy a house or a car, you can't do anything but work at every dead-end job you can squeeze into twenty-four hours. And when that's not enough, there's the Common and guys like Anthony and guys like Dave to tell you how awful it is. "What do you want?" I asked after going down and blocking Anthony's path.

"I want you to leave me alone."

"What am I doing to you?"

"This," he said, pointing at the sidewalk between us. "This. Me. You and me. The fact that I'm me and you're you and I'm here doing this with you even though I never do things like this. You think this is easy? You think I want to be doing this? You think I've got time for this?"

I must have looked incredulous because he responded by clenching his fists and tightening his shoulders and arms as if ready to strike me.

"I wouldn't do that."

"Why not?"

"We've got company," I said, looking back at my apartment. It was on the third floor, and my roommates were at the windows making a series of indecent gestures.

"You live together? People like you? They let you live together?"

"Nobody else wants to live with us."

"But you can do anything you want."

"Pretty much."

"That's disgusting."

"Sometimes. Yeah. It can get a little wild. But sometimes it's fun, and sometimes it's just living the way anybody lives, and sometimes it can save you."

"What do you mean?"

"I mean when someone comes into your neighborhood and tries to frighten you."

"People do that?"

"Isn't that what you're doing?"

"No," he said, looking hurt. "I want to talk. I want you to give me a chance to talk. I want you to stop running away every time I find you."

I was talking to two different people. One Anthony had gone to the Common; the other knew nothing about it. One Anthony thought he was following me; the other thought I was following him. One of them would start talking and then stop, terrified, as if the other had him by the throat, and then it would happen again, only the other way around.

"I want to explain what happened that day," he told me, although he was clearly telling himself. "I was taking a walk. I was minding my own business."

"And mine," I said.

"You calling me a faggot?"

"I'm not calling you anything. I'm just saying that I was there and you were there and we talked about sex and how much it would cost—"

"—a theoretical question which anybody in a free country can ask."

"After which we went to a hotel."

"After which you went to a hotel and I walked, by coincidence, in the direction of the hotel. You can't prove anything."

"Look," I said. "I don't want to prove anything. Whatever did or didn't happen that day, I just want it to be over."

"You do?"

"Sometimes you do things you don't understand," I continued. "It happens to me. It happens to you. It happens to everybody. And maybe they happen again, and maybe they happen once and that's the end of it. I don't know. But I know I don't like being followed, and you're telling me you don't like following me, or waiting for me to follow you, or whatever's going on, so let's just stop it. O.K.?"

"You won't tell anybody?"

"No."

"And you won't hate me?"

I lied and told him I wouldn't, and, before I could stop him, he told me his name. "I'm Anthony," he said, putting his hand out. "Anthony D'Ambrosio."

He said that he hadn't slept. He said that he hadn't done any work. He said that he was an eighth grade math teacher in Melrose and hadn't graded any homework or made any class plans or written any tests.

Then he realized what he'd done.

"Oh no!" he cried, pulling his hand back as if from fire. "You tricked me! You fooled me into telling you all that!"

"I've already forgotten," I promised.

But it was too late. He turned around and ran from me and my roommates so fast that he ran right out of his hat. Even then, there seemed to be two of him, running at different speeds or in different directions. The result was a gait so spastic it shook his hat and most of one boot off, and, when he turned to retrieve the hat, something landed on his head. Benny had filled some condoms with water and opened a window and was using them as bombs, one of which hit me and one of which hit Anthony. He was so startled, he screamed and fell and got up and fell again, without being hit, just falling over himself or his two selves or however many of them there were until finally, barely, he was up, and that was it. All that remained of Anthony, Food of the Gods, was what lay behind him on the sidewalk, his ridiculous fur hat and a selection of broken and unbroken rubbers.

"What are we going to do?" he asked when he called the next day.

"Who is this?" I demanded, although I had a pretty good idea. He must have come back and looked at the names on the door.

"This is Anthony, and I'm calling about my hat. I need it back."

"Should I mail it?"

"Too risky."

"Do you want to come get it?"

"Riskier."

"And you can't do without it . . ."

"Not a chance," he said. "My wife would find out." And then, as if I'd asked him to, he told me the whole story.

He'd met her in Italy, in Abruzzo. He was there for a wedding and was introduced by a cousin. A nice girl, they told him. Someone to keep a nice house and to raise some nice kids and to give a man a nice life. Nice. He said the word as if it were a swear word. He said her name as if it were a joke. But he loved her. Oh, yes. And his kids, a boy and a girl, the best kids in the world. The boy had attention problems but was improving with the help of a specialist, and he'd pitched one and a half hitless innings against the team that went on to finish second in the nine-and-ten-year-old division of the Melrose Little League. He was taking trumpet lessons and could play a piece called "Bugler's Revenge," which was, in Anthony's opinion, a piece only a much older child should be playing. And his daughter played the piano and was president of the Busy Bee's, a social club for seventh graders who got B or better on their last two report cards. The trouble was that his wife took the credit and turned them against him. She told them he didn't care, not about them, not about her, not about anything but himself.

"Do you think that's fair?" he asked. "I make all the money. I fix everything around the house that needs fixing. I cut the lawn and shovel the snow and keep the car running. I can't watch T.V. once in a while? I can't sit down and drink a beer?"

It would have surprised me if I hadn't heard it before.

The wife who doesn't love me, who doesn't understand me because I won't tell her or myself who I actually am. Anthony was saying what, in my experience, closeted men always say when given the chance.

Then he said what I was dreading.

"I want to try again."

"No," I replied, forgetting what *my* wife had said. Another late payment and she'd cut my visitation. "—no, unless you meet my original price," I added. It was fifty, and he met it without question, as well as all my expectations. To call what Anthony and I did the next afternoon sex would be generous, but it was sweet and it was, thankfully, brief, and I trusted him enough to use my apartment the next time we met. And then, one day, he asked if we could do it every day.

"What about the missus?"

"She's in Italy for the summer, with the kids. I stayed home to teach summer school. Because of the time difference, she can't call after seven or before about twelve."

Sounds like the perfect set up. I somehow managed to say that.

But it wasn't so bad.

He'd come over, and we'd go to my room, and, after, he'd pay me, and then, until he had to go home, he'd follow me around and ask questions. How do you know if you're gay? When did you know? Was it all at once or a little at a time, and what did it feel like, and what does it feel like now? Do you feel any different? Do you feel like the rest of you is different? Do you think you're a woman? He was asking about homosexual feelings, but, really, he was asking about any feelings, of any kind. After a lifetime of being told by his family and his church and his country what to feel and when and how much, he wanted to know how people had feelings, how they said what they thought and did what they wanted, how they got away with it but, also, how they did it in the first place. And then he'd call us jerks.

"You know what's wrong with you guys?"

We'd be sitting in the living room. He'd be sitting on the couch in his underpants. "What?" one of us would eventually reply.

"You guys are more interested in feeling good than in doing good."

"Don't forget looking good."

"Is there even one of you that can factor a binomial? Is there one of you who can look at a graph and determine the equation that produced it?"

"If a train leaves Kansas City at six in the morning, how long does it take a fairy in Omaha to make himself come?"

"You see!" he'd shout as if he hadn't made the same point the night before and all the nights before that. "How is this country going to keep its place in the world if we don't have people who can do math? How are we going to build our roads? How are we going to maintain the roads we already have?"

He called us fags, fairies, perverts, and queens. He called us un-American and un-Christian and psychologically un-developed.

So we called him—Anthony. That seemed insult enough.

He was every gym teacher who'd made fun of us. He was every guidance counselor who'd given up on us and every youth minister who hadn't. Anthony was a chance to persecute a world that was still, for the most part, persecuting us.

But one day I walked in, and he was in the living room, naked except for his hat. He was going from one of my roommates to the other, doing whatever they commanded. It was a game called The Receiving Line, and I'd seen it before. I'd done it before, and I thought, at first, that I was looking at a new, less ambivalent

Anthony. But he wasn't laughing or even smiling, and he didn't appear to be drunk. He looked frightened, and I asked what was going on, and Dave told me as if he were in no way involved. Anthony had made his mother's puttanesca and had, in the classic style, garnished rather than smothered the pasta, and Benny had complained. He'd said that Anthony was scrimping, and Anthony had said that Benny was ignorant, and things would have been fine or, at least, no worse than usual if Benny hadn't been dumped by his boyfriend, Ken. It was for the third or fourth time, but Benny was upset and took Anthony's criticism so personally a dish and several punches were thrown after which Benny told Anthony to bend over. When Anthony refused, Benny threatened to call the Melrose school district, and, by the time I arrived, Tim and Shawn, a friend of Tim's, and Marshall, a friend of Shawn's, and Dave were alternately participating and pretending they weren't, pretending to stand back and be disgusted, and I told them all to get out.

"He had it coming," said Benny.

"He's bleeding," I replied. "Look at him. Look what you've done to him."

Blood was running from Anthony's anus down his leg, and there was blood and shit on the couch and the chairs and the only decent rug in the apartment.

"I'm not going anywhere," said Dave. "I live here."

"Not tonight."

"Where do you suggest that I go?"

"Try hell," I answered. And he left. They all did.

We were building a New Jerusalem, and its rules, however few, had to be obeyed. You could do drugs, but not too many. You could prostitute yourself but not too often and not too cheaply. You could sleep with your friend's boyfriend, but not the boyfriend of a good friend, and you could sleep with someone underage, but only a little underage and only if he lied well enough to confuse a reasonable person even if the reasonable person wasn't you. But taking advantage of the fear we all lived under was different. It was wrong, and they knew it, and they accepted their punishment in order to feel as well as to know that it was wrong.

"This is pretty bad," I said as I tended to Anthony with some gauze I found in the bathroom. "I think you need the hospital."

"I can't," he replied.

"Why not? You need somebody to get you there? You need somebody to pay?"

"I need somebody to get me home. My wife is coming home. She and the kids are probably there already."

Marshall was studying art history at Harvard, and he was rich, and he was beautiful. "I'm sorry," he said when I saw him the next morning.

I was on my way to the salon. He was on his way to Cambridge.

"You were drunk."

"Not that drunk. I feel terrible. What a mess."

"He'll be all right."

"I don't know."

"What do you mean?"

"He loves you."

"Are you sure?"

"As sure as I am that Michelangelo painted the Sistine Chapel."

"Did he?" I asked, only half joking. Then I had an idea. "I suppose, at some level, I love him too," I said.

"You do?"

"Sure," I continued, trying to sound more interesting than I was. It was the only shot I had at a guy like Marshall. "I mean, there's love and there's love, isn't there? I mean, there's the love you feel for a lover, and the love you feel for an old lover who's a friend, and the love you feel for an old lover who's no longer a friend. And then there's the love you feel for someone because you know them in some stupid way like the way I know Anthony . . ."

"And then there's ears," Marshall replied.

"Excuse me?"

We were standing at the corner of my street and his, and people stepped around us as Marshall explained what he called the telescoping of generations. He said that people are attracted by physical traits they recognize as familiar because of some feature of their mother's or father's or grandfather's face, or their great-

great grandfather's face, someone they'd never seen or even heard about. He said that certain ways of seeing are innate and therefore inherited, which means, he said as I noticed my bus come and go, that we could be attracted to a certain forehead or jaw or, yes, ears because that's what was considered beautiful in whatever tribe or tribes our ancestors are from. He went on about art, about the relationship between seeing and art, and I didn't really follow, but I didn't really care. Everything Marshall said was art. It all sounded like music or poetry, even what he said when he swore or complained or that morning when someone, hurrying past, ran into him. "You could watch where you're walking." If I'd said it, it would have sounded like what it was, an insult. When he said it, it sounded like a suggestion, an appeal to a fellow citizen's more courteous side.

"Anthony's in love with me because his great grandfather and I have the same ears?"

"Or his great grandmother or his aunt or his uncle or some orangutan that loved some other orangutan ten million years ago."

"I think Anthony looks more like a gorilla than an orangutan."

"Don't be rude," he scolded, taking my chin and turning it from side to side.

"What do you think?"

"Pointy."

"Is that good?"

"It's great," he said and gave me a wink that nearly sent me to the ground.

His bus came, and he got on, and I waited for mine in such a daze I nearly missed it again. I went to work and did my job and, after, my other job, but the whole time I was still with Marshall. I was feeling his hand on my chin and remembering his attention to my ears and to my self-serving philosophizing about Anthony until, a week later, when Anthony called and I met him at a Dunkin' Donuts in the Combat Zone. He wants to start over, I told an imaginary Marshall as Anthony told me. He wants to be friends. Just friends. No sex. No money.

"Just coffee," the real Marshall said when I saw him at a birthday party for Paul. "What are you going to do?"

"Be his friend."

"You think you can do that?"

"I can try," I replied, interested only in friendship with Marshall.

He'd come with Shawn and went over to him, and they left. But the next day he called and invited me to a show at the Museum of Fine Arts. We went the only Friday night I could get off, and by then I'd met with Anthony again, this time for a walk along the waterfront.

"Do you think he's dangerous?" Marshall asked as we ate in the museum's cafeteria.

"Isn't everybody?"

He looked at me, and I thought I'd been discovered. "Are you—involved?"

"With Anthony?"

"With anyone."

I was seeing a man named Michael. "No," I said. "And you?"

"I've been seeing Shawn. He's nice, but . . ."

"He's got the wrong ears. And it's complicated because you've got the right ears for him. It's tough to be an orangutan."

Marshall responded with a confession. He'd had all the breaks, he said. He'd been to the right schools and had known all the right people and had traveled to all the right places. He'd even been born to the right family. They were fine with his orientation. They'd paid for therapy to help him adjust. But still he was lacking. There was some depth, some emotional honesty he hadn't experienced until that night with Anthony. "You were brilliant," he said.

"I just said what I thought."

"That's what I mean. I don't know anyone who can do that. I can't do it myself."

He got our bill and, over my objections, paid it and took me to a room of what I now know to be Impressionists.

"Is this the show?" I asked.

"Forget the show. I want you to see something."

"What?"

"This," he said when we got to a painting of three sunflowers in a vase. "I want you to look at this and tell me what it means."

"Well," I began. "It's flowers . . ."

"Yes."

"And the flowers are in a vase. Or maybe it's a jug . . ."

"Yes."

"And the jug is green. And the wall . . . the wall behind the jug . . . it's green, but a different green. And the table the jug is on . . . it's brown."

"I think you're getting there."

But the table was brown in some places and purple in others. And one of the flowers looked like a flower, and one of them looked like the idea of a flower—some idea the painter got while looking at a flower—and one of them looked like it was in the wrong painting. It looked bigger than the others, or brighter, or painted with different paint or from a different perspective, and the jug was only painted on one side. It looked like it was about to fall over, into the table, which was also leaning as was the wall, as was I by the time I told Marshall the truth.

"Anthony," I said. "That's who I am. That's who this painting says I am."

I felt dizzy and found a place to sit down and closed my eyes, and, when that didn't help, I put my head between my knees. "So much for being brilliant."

"You looked at a painting and had a reaction. That's what the painter was hoping."

"That I'd pass out?"

"Something like that," Marshall replied, putting his arm around me for what might have been a minute or might have been an hour. I remember wondering when the museum closed.

But when we got home, I saw Anthony again. He was waiting in my apartment.

"Tim, let me in," he said when I turned on the light.

"Why are you here?"

"To tell you."

"To tell me what?"

"That I did what you said. Just like you said."

I tried to remember our last conversation. I'd barely been listening. I'd been watching Marshall watching me listen.

"You told me to leave Angela."

"No, I didn't."

"You told me to make a choice."

"Not that choice. Not yet."

"I love you," he said. And the jug fell over.

"I don't love you, Anthony. I'll never love you. I'm sorry."

I checked the obituaries in the *Globe* the next morning and every morning after that for a month and a half. I read about a woman who worked for thirty-eight years as a crossing guard and a man who swam with Esther Williams. I read about the inventor of *Jeopardy!* and a contributor of three new words to *The Oxford English Dictionary* and the first person to grow a carrot in space. And since I was buying the paper anyway, I read the rest: about the talks between Anwar Sadat and Moshe Dayan; about the riots in Turkey, and the outlawing of fluorocarbons, and the rise of Japan, and the decline of Sid Vicious, and the Red Sox blowing a fourteen-game lead to lose that year's pennant race to the Yankees. I read about the Southwest Corridor Project. A group of citizens in Jamaica Plain had rallied against the destruction of their neighborhood by a six-lane highway and got the governor to reallocate the funds for a commuter train. I'd never been to Jamaica Plain and didn't care, but it made me happy. Power to the people and all that.

And then, one day, there he was.

ANTHONY D'AMBROSIO

Of Melrose, age 34, went to the arms of Our Maker November 16 after a brief illness. Beloved husband of Angela D'Ambrosio. Devoted father of daughter, Christine, and son, Anthony Jr. Also survived by brothers, Marco and Richard, and sister, Patricia, and mother, Marguerite. Anthony will be remembered for his service to a generation of students in the Melrose Public Schools and his fundraising for both the Jimmy Fund and the American Cancer Society. Visitation from 2 until 4 P.M. Friday at Bottari and Sons Funeral Home. A Mass of Christian Burial will be held Saturday at St. Mary's Catholic Church, 12 Lichter Street in Melrose at 10 A.M. and interment will follow at Holy Cross Cemetery in Malden. Donations may be made to the Anthony D'Ambrosio Math Education Fund at P.O. Box 1996, Melrose, MA 02148.

Had he killed himself and the family didn't want to say? Had he worried himself into a heart attack or an ulcer or a stroke or been distracted and fallen downstairs or driven his car into a tree? Tim and Benny and I wanted to go to his service if only to find out but decided that unwise. Instead, we had our own service, and, instead of Anthony, we buried his hat. It was hanging from a hook in the front hall, and we took it and a trowel and dug a hole near the bench where Anthony and I met. We put the hat in and covered it and said a few words, and I sometimes went back although I never again tricked. I took Anthony's advice and thought about doing good instead of feeling good. I took out a loan and got a degree and a job and went to the bench when I wanted to remember Anthony and, when they too were in the *Globe*, all the others.

Benny. David. Carlos, a guy who worked at the salon.

And then it was my beloved Marshall, although he was by that time living and teaching in Chicago. I heard it from a friend of a friend of the man Marshall left me for, and, for a while, it felt as if Marshall had left me again. It felt as if everyone had left, as if everyone I knew was dead or dying, and there was nothing I could do until, in 1985, they came up with a test and there was one thing I had to do.

"Who is this?" Angela asked me as I had asked Anthony.

I found her number in the phonebook. There were several D'Ambrosios but only two with the letter A. "I was a friend of your husband's," I said to the second A after the first one hung up, and, for a moment, there was nothing. Then we spoke as if she'd known me for years, which, apparently, she had.

"Why are you calling me now?"

"Because there's a test now. You might be infected."

"Are you infected?"

"No."

"Then how could he be infected?"

"He was with other men, and they were infected."

"They?"

"Three."

"Mother of God . . ."

"It was an experiment."

"It was a sin," she said. "He shouldn't be buried in the cemetery. I shouldn't be buried with him. His children shouldn't be with him."

I thought she was going to say that I had ruined her life. Instead, she asked if Anthony had loved me.

"He was confused," I replied.

"By what?"

"By everything. I don't think he was gay, Mrs. D'Ambrosio. I think he was angry. I think he was getting even with somebody."

"With me?"

"With somebody before you. With somebody before any of us."

I said this and waited again, after which she asked if the two of us could meet. She wanted to move on and thought meeting me would help. She named a restaurant in Melrose and promised to come alone, but I was worried and said so. She might bring friends. She might bring Anthony's brothers. They might jump me in the parking lot or follow me home and beat me up there. I suggested a restaurant in the city, and it was her turn to be afraid. I might bring my fellow degenerates, and who knew what they might do?

"What about the bench?"

I don't remember if I said it or she did, but I remember that she said the time and that I agreed to the time and that I got to the bench well before the time.

"Yo! Dude!"

A pair of boys went by on skateboards. They were the same age as Anthony's boy, I thought after doing the math. I wondered if he still played baseball. I wondered if he still played the trumpet or if his sister still played the piano. I wondered about my own children.

My wife had remarried. I saw them twice a month with court ordered supervision.

"Do that again, and I'll smack you."

There was a woman and a much younger boy on the next bench. When he wouldn't behave, the woman threatened him.

"O.K.," she said. "Mommy's going to leave you here."

I watched a man read a book as he walked down Tremont Street. I watched a couple buy a pretzel from a vendor near the Park Street M.B.T.A. station. The woman took half and gave the man half, and they walked to the Frog Pond, not talking, just walking along eating their halves. I watched a man climb a tree and a woman teach a child to ride a bike and another teach a dog to catch a Frisbee. I watched a man collect bottles. He went from garbage can to garbage can taking bottles that he put in a grocery cart that was overflowing with bottles.

And later, so much later that Angela wasn't coming—that she'd never been coming, I realized—there was another man.

He passed me once and then again and then sat down and said the code.

"Nice day," he said, which, when I looked, I noticed that it was.

It was April. It was warm. The sun was out for the first time all spring, and the man wanted people to be glad.

The
Field of
Machpelah

Josh returned from his midnight rounds at the cemetery to find a late-model Volvo idling outside the cemetery gate. Was the driver lost? he wondered as he considered the car from the cemetery's security car, inside the gate. Should he wait for whomever it was to back up and drive away? Should he do something more? Unable to see the occupant or occupants, he eased the security car a few feet forward, and then again, and then he activated the car's emergency light. When there was still no response, he activated the car's public address system, filling the night with short bursts of static by turning the system on and off until, frustrated, he drove to the guardhouse at one side of the gate and got out and flipped the switch for the light on the gate.

And there he was: not a carful of murderous thugs but an old man. He sat in the driver's seat, holding the wheel with his right hand while fumbling with his left to open the window.

"The cemetery's closed," Josh told him when, with a whine, the glass lowered.

"As it must be, of course."

"Then what do you want?"

"To come in, if possible. To convince you to let me in."

"How do you plan to do that?"

The man smiled, and Josh noticed that he wore no hat and no coat although it was March and only forty degrees.

"By telling you about my wife," said the man. "By telling you that she's over at the hospital and she's dying and they want to stop her machines."

"So?"

"So, I want to know where she'll go. I want to see the place before I give my permission."

"You can do that tomorrow, in the daytime."

"I've seen it in the daytime already. I've seen it plenty. We both have. I want to see it when it's dark, when it's scary. I'm sure you understand."

"No," said Josh, at which point the man got out and came toward the tall, iron bars that kept them apart.

"You're going to let me in," said the man. "I know you are. And I know something more. Something here, something right here. What is it?"

He looked at the bars. He looked at the car, at his car and then Josh's car, through the bars. Then he looked at Josh as if seeing him for the first time.

"It's you," he said. "You don't belong here either."

And what could Josh say?

He'd gone to Brown, intending to become a doctor like his father and brother but had dropped out and traveled for a year and then worked for a year. He'd moved to Boston and tried restaurant work and then driving a taxi and then data entry and telephone solicitation and then selling clothes. To make rent, he'd worked two and sometimes three jobs at once and still hadn't made it and was about to give up when he re-met a girl named Rochelle. He'd met her at the restaurant and re-met her at a party, and, once they were going out, she called a cousin who called a friend who called another friend who knew about a job that made Josh laugh when he heard. The graveyard shift at the graveyard. Guarding Forest Hills Cemetery from eleven to seven, five nights a week for twelve dollars an hour. Rather than serve people food or drive them around Boston or to the airport, he drove around the underworld, night after night, halting his progress along one or another of Alexander Dearborn's ghost-filled thoroughfares to explain himself to the ghosts who were famous. Eugene O'Neill. Anne Sexton. Edward Everett Hale. William Lloyd Garrison. e.e. cummings. And a smattering of Massachusetts governors, Revolutionary and Civil War heroes, and—safely dead—several famous doctors. He told them about the B he got in Genetics because the professor was a jerk and the C he got in Organic Chemistry because the professor was an even bigger jerk and because the secret to getting an A was to put all the reactions on flash cards and drill them for an hour twice a day, which nobody had told him. His only hope was to have some interesting foreign travel or community service to put on his application or some professor who'd liked him enough to write the sort of recommendation that Amy, his girlfriend at the time, had gotten from her psychology professor. She'd done a research project on the effect of antidepressants on learning behavior in rats, and it had led to a paper on which, thanks to the professor, she'd been listed as first author. She'd suggested that Josh take antidepressants. Maybe it would help your grades, she'd said. And then he'd whiffed the M.C.A.T., which had put the matter beyond question. Rather than apply and get into a school even worse than the third-tier safety school his brother had gotten into or, more likely, nowhere at all, he'd decided to cut bait, to make a virtue of his failure, to see it as evidence of an unruly genius for which the famous of Forest Hills expressed, when he paused at their monuments, silent admiration.

"Can I just stay where I am?" the man continued, his head now to one side. "It won't be the same, but it's better than nothing."

"We have to get traffic through here."

"I thought you were closed?"

"Emergency traffic. A fire truck if we need one. An ambulance if a gang of kids comes over the fence and somebody gets hurt."

"Can I park on the drive, maybe up near the road?"

"I'd rather you didn't. There's stuff up there."

"What kind of stuff?"

"Night stuff. Gay stuff. Cruising. That kind of stuff. I don't want the cemetery to be responsible."

"Will you call the police?"

"I might."

"And will they come?"

Josh didn't think so, but he couldn't admit it. "I'm asking you to leave," he said, and the man shrugged and returned to his still-running car, which he backed up and turned around and drove toward the road, although he didn't go to the road. He went a short way down the cemetery drive and stopped and turned his motor and all but his parking lights off, and Josh went to his car and called Rochelle on his cell. "Had a little excitement tonight," he said when she answered. "A guy came to the gate and asked to be let in. He wanted to see his wife's grave."

"He hasn't seen it before?"

"She isn't dead. She's about to be dead. He wanted to see where she'll go."

"Why can't he do that in the daytime?"

"That was my point."

"And?"

"He said he's seen it in the daytime. He said they both have. He wanted to see it at night, in the dark."

". . . when it's scary," said Rochelle.

"Not you too."

"I don't know, Josh. I think it's sweet. I think you should have let him."

My brother would have let him. She didn't say it, but Josh could hear it in her tone. Danny the cop. Danny the angel. The brother she'd marry if it wasn't prohibited by the Catholic priests she otherwise ignored.

"I've been overruled," he told the man after opening the gate and driving out to where he was waiting. "So where is this gig?"

"At the corner of Oleander and Verbena Paths."

"Where's that?"

"Across from the Field of Machpelah."

"Where's that?"

"You know Chestnut Avenue? You know where Chestnut Avenue meets Fountain Avenue? You know the road that runs along the fountain side of Lake Hibiscus?"

He'd pulled beside the man and lowered his window as had the man, and the two of them were talking as he'd sometimes talked to other cabbies. His fare would be screaming about a flight or a meeting he'd miss if Josh didn't figure out where he was, and he'd pull up to another cab and hope the driver was friendly and spoke English and that the light didn't change. "I'll follow you," he said, finally. "But I'm putting myself on the line, so it's in and out, you got it? Five minutes. And you don't tell anybody. Not the doctors. Not the nurses. Not your family or friends. Not even . . ."

". . . my wife?" said the man, smiling again. "The doctors tell me that she has no detectable brain activity, so don't worry. I couldn't tell her if I wanted to. But she knows," he said. "And she appreciates it. We both do. I'm sorry, but could I possibly ask your name?"

"Josh."

"Short for Joshua. How perfect." He motioned toward the gate that now loomed before them both. "You play the trumpet, Josh?"

"Excuse me?"

" 'Seven priests bearing seven trumpets circled Jericho for seven days and then, when Joshua gave the order, the people shouted and the wall came down.' It's a great story and a great name. 'The Lord is my salvation.' That's what your name means, Josh. Did you know?"

It was as if the man were from another world, as if while sitting beside his moribund wife he'd had some glimpse of the divine and would be, ever after, a little off. He spoke as if listening and moved as if controlled, and what he said seemed right but also slightly unreal, slightly more or less than human. Or maybe he was crazy. Maybe they both were, Josh thought as he turned around and followed him back to the gate. How else to explain the risk he was taking for someone he didn't know and would never see again? How else to explain that before re-entering the gate, he extinguished his headlights and the light on the gate, that he did so at the man's suggestion to defeat the camera on the gate? And how to explain the hallucinations? As they drove, the extra set of headlights struck the double and triple rows of headstones in ways that made unfamiliar shadows run toward or away or along beside them, and, once, Josh thought he heard a shout. Once, he thought he saw a coyote; they sometimes took refuge in the cemetery's 275 forested acres. And, once, he nearly hit the man. He saw a shadow that looked like a pair of kids running along the lake and kept driving after the man had stopped to turn a corner.

"Five minutes," Josh reminded him when they arrived, saying it on the loudspeaker rather than getting out.

It was cemetery policy. After dark, he was to spot trouble and to report it. He was to stay in the cruiser at all times, under all circumstances.

Besides, Rochelle had called twice and was calling again. "Josh? Is that you?"

"Yo!"

"I was worried."

"About what?"

"About you."

"What about me?"

"I called, and you didn't answer, and I got scared. I remembered what I'd asked you to do, and I felt responsible. I'm sorry," she said.

Yo! Josh said again, this time to himself.

Amy would get him in scrapes like this and say that she hadn't, that she'd only been expressing her opinion and he could have objected at any time. Sure. Any time he wanted about a three-hour lecture on the history of women's rights. Any time he wanted to hear what a heartless, insensitive cretin he was and probably always would be. Any time he wanted to go without sex until he came up with an apology that satisfied her and her sister and her mother and all her friends. Rochelle wasn't the sharpest tool in the shed. She might, in fact, be a little dumb. But there was smart and there was smart, and Rochelle was the kind of smart that made everything easy when she was around. When Josh told her about Brown, about quitting while Amy continued and got into the med school at Brown and two others, Rochelle said it didn't matter. She said that he could be a nurse. She talked about the two of them becoming nurses, about each of them taking turns to put the other through school until they both had degrees and could work as much or as little as they needed to raise a couple of kids in a nice house in a nice town with good enough schools and maybe take vacations with Danny and his family. She talked about movies that were funny and clothes that were popular and money as if it were a nice thing to have, which wouldn't impress Amy, but who cared about her?

"I gave him five minutes."

"How long has it been?"

Josh looked at his watch. "One," he said. "One and a half."

"Four more and you can forget the whole thing until you come home and find me in bed."

"Where are you now?"

"At the restaurant. I'm cashing out."

"You'll be tired."

"Not that tired. And I can go back to sleep if I want. I don't work tomorrow. We can sleep the whole day if we want."

At the man's request, he'd turned his lights off, again, as had the man. The man wanted an authentic experience and Josh wanted an anonymous experience, to avoid discovery at any cost, so he sat in his car and considered the numbers that glowed on his watch.

"So how was the restaurant?"

"O.K."

"Only O.K.?"

"It was one of those nights that started slow and got busy."

"Just when you were ready to go home."

"Just when you were O.K. with no money but leaving a little early at least and then you had to stay for not that much money anyway. I had three parties of two and all they wanted was coffee and dessert and to sit there talking about every little thing that ever happened to them."

"And then they gave you a buck."

"Maybe. One of them didn't tip me at all."

"You're kidding."

"I'm serious. I couldn't believe it."

Three minutes.

"And then there was this guy."

"What kind of guy?"

"You know. One of those guys who comes in with a bunch of other guys and they're all drunk, and there's one guy who wants to show off."

"What'd he do?"

"He said stuff."

"What kind of stuff?"

"You know. Stupid stuff. Drunk stuff."

"What'd he say? What'd Brian say? Was he the manager tonight?"

Two minutes. One.

"Time's up!" Josh called a few seconds early. But the man didn't answer. And when Josh looked, he couldn't see him. "Oh Christ!" he said when he turned his lights on and looked again.

"What's the matter?"

"He's on the ground. He collapsed. What do I do now?"

Afraid that he'd have to do mouth to mouth, Josh leapt from the car and ran to the man only to have him roll over and ask a question.

"Do you know what the Field of Machpelah is?"

"Part of the cemetery?"

"No. What it really is. What this part of the cemetery is named for."

"Maybe another time . . ."

"It's the field Abraham bought from Ephron the Hittite for four hundred shekels and where he asked his son Isaac to bury him with his wife Sarah and where Isaac's son Jacob buried him with his wife Rebecca and where Jacob's sons buried him with his wife Leah. They're the three great married couples of history, the heroes of conjugal combat, the mighty men and women who grabbed shield and sword and strode fearless into that inglorious and never-ending engagement." The man raised one and then the other of his arms. "I thought I told you to get some milk on the way home!" he exclaimed, frowning at his right arm as if watching it speak. "Don't talk to me in that tone! I do as much for this family as you, maybe more!" he continued, frowning at his left before frowning, again, at his right. "I asked you for milk, not to donate a kidney!" Then he rested his arms on his chest and looked at Josh. "Did you know that the Torah says it is a man's responsibility to keep his wife sexually satisfied? It's true. Ask any Jew. It might have to be one you know pretty well, but go ahead. Ask. And you know what they get for their trouble? The same thing anybody gets. The same thing the patriarchs got. This," he said indicating the dirt that had gotten on his hands, on his face, on his clothes when he'd thrown himself on the grave. "It's the same thing I got from forty-three years of keeping Edith satisfied. And I did. I asked her the other day, and she told me. Of course, you never know with the ladies. Not for sure. They sometimes tell you things just to make you feel good. But I did my best. And I did my best for Fletcher, White, & McKenna for almost as long. You never heard of them just like you never heard of me and Edith, and you know why? Because I had a job, and I did it and did it right, and, when you do that, nobody knows anything about you. But I know you, Josh. And now you know me, so I think we should celebrate." He sat up and got to his knees and dug at the earth with his hands. "Don't worry," he said when they were full of dirt and he'd climbed to his feet and started toward Josh holding his hands like a bowl and the dirt like an offering. "It's a wedding present. It's for you and that girl you keep calling. I know your name, mighty Joshua. What's hers?"

"Rochelle," Josh replied, hoping that there was still some chance, however small, that he could get the man out of there.

"Rochelle, from the old French for rock. No wonder you turn to her when you're scared. It's a good thing to have a rock. I had a rock. I had Edith. Do you know what Edith means?" The man stopped about three feet from Josh. He looked at his hands. He looked at the dirt in his hands and then opened them and let the dirt fall to the ground. "I need to get back to the Brigham," he muttered. He looked as he had at the gate, as he first had. He looked old. He looked lost.

"Do you think you can drive?" Josh asked, guiding him back through the stones.

"I think so. And it isn't far. It's just up the road. It's just . . ."

"Up the Jamaicaway," said Josh. "You turn left at the end of the drive and stay straight until you get to Longwood Avenue, and then you turn right and you're there. You think you can do that?"

The headlights on his car were aimed at the man's car, and, had he looked inside, Josh would have seen the boy before he and the man arrived at the driver's side door. Suddenly, the door flew open and the boy jumped out, upending the man and leaving Josh to stare openmouthed as the boy disappeared and the cruiser came to life and shot off, driven by another boy. By the time he realized that the boys were the shadows he'd seen by the lake, the car was roaring through the night, brightening this and then that group of leafless trees as it started and stopped and then stopped for a long time before starting again with what sounded like the laughter of several boys. At one point, Josh worried that it might come back, that among the erratic looping circuits the car made through the cemetery's landscaped hills would be one that brought it past or even directly into him and the man. But the car continued, sometimes squealing as if on asphalt and sometimes grinding as if through section after section of the sanctified turf until, again, the car stopped and started, but, this time, there was an enormous splash.

"Mister?"

Josh had checked to be sure the man was breathing and that his neck was straight or at least pretty straight and then that he moved, at one time or another, all his limbs.

But as he reached to help the man up, the man pulled away.

"Who are you?" he snapped.

"It's me. Josh. Joshua. You're at Forest Hills."

"What am I doing here?" the man demanded as he rose. "Why did you bring me here?"

"I didn't bring you anywhere."

"You're lying! You kidnapped me! You're trying to kill me! You're trying to rape me! You said so yourself! There's stuff here! Night stuff! Gay stuff! You don't want to be responsible! That's what you said, and now I know why! Get away from me!"

The man turned, as if to run, and Josh reached for him and held his arm until he heard something snap and let the man go.

"You've broken it!" the man howled.

"I didn't mean to."

"It doesn't matter! I'll have you arrested! I'll see you in jail! Wait until my children hear about this!"

The man turned and, again, started away, and Josh followed him, trotting down the road, asking for the man to stop until he saw someone else on the road. The cemetery was full of statues, and, as the man passed what appeared to be another person, Josh thought it was a statue, then that it was one of the boys and that the boy might strike the man. But the figure considered the man and then turned to consider Josh. It seemed to float as much as walk toward Josh, and, for the first time in all his months at Forest Hills, he wondered if there were, in fact, ghosts at the cemetery. With all the other arrivals and departures, he wondered, again, if one of the night's departures had been his mind until the figure was close enough that he could see not a boy or another man but a woman and then that it was a woman he knew. He hadn't answered his phone for so long, she'd driven to the place in the fence they used when she met him to skinny-dip in the lake or to smoke a joint on top of Anne Sexton or e.e. cummings or to have sex in the security car with the loudspeaker on or, once, on top of Edward Everett Hale. She'd walked to the corner of Oleander and Verbena Paths and had heard the man and then him and then had seen and walked toward him because she had a plan, Josh thought, because she always had a plan, or Danny did, or he would when she called him and asked what to tell the police when they arrived. She'd say that the man had been crazy from the start. She'd say that he'd tricked him into opening the gate and, as soon as he had, had tried to run him over. She'd say something. Anything. One way or another she'd make it O.K., Josh thought as the ghost stopped and reached for him the way Sarah reached for Abraham before Abraham was Abraham, back when he was a twenty-two-year-old almost-Abraham wondering what the hell to do next.

"Josh," asked Rochelle, "is that you?"

Home Depot

You know how it is. You're married, you're married to Albie forty-two—what is it?—forty-three years, so at least you know Albie. Right?

But one day, we're upstairs. We're lying in bed because it's Saturday and it's July and everybody else is out mowing grass but we're retired so what do we care? We're lying there, and the phone rings, so I think it's my daughter, Chris. She's pregnant, but she's forty, and it's her first, so she's acting like a kid, she's acting like she's the baby. "I felt a kick," she calls to tell me every maybe five or ten minutes. "I felt it here. I felt it there. You think the baby could be breech? You think the baby could be something else?" Mother of God! I'll give *her* a kick if she calls me again. Albie, I say. Get up and get the phone because it's Chris. Get it downstairs so I don't have to hear, I tell him, even though I know I'm going to lie there listening to him as he listens to her. Oh Chris, I hear him say, and I'm thinking, *Oh Chris what?* I'll split if I don't find out. And then the house splits. BLAM! It's the furnace. It bangs when it comes on. BLAM! BLAM! BLAM! I've been telling Albie for two years. I'm halfway down the stairs when I remember, it's July, it's hot, so it can't be the furnace. It's Albie. I can see him in the kitchen. He's banging the phone on the wall. What are you doing that for? I'm asking until he turns and says he can't tell me, he can't tell anybody. Call Chris, he says, but I tell him, how can I? You broke the f-ing telephone.

Excuse me. But you say what you have to say.

And you let your man cry. You let him cry at funerals, weddings, all the other stuff. Fine. I tell Albie he can cry, and then I tell him he can stop. That's enough, Albie. You take what God gives you, and you do what you can. *The amnio was positive.* He says it like it's my fault. He says it like this time he can't stop crying, he'll never stop. So I tell him, so? So, the baby's going to look funny? So, the baby's going to act funny? So, the baby's going to grow up and be a kid that people notice at the shopping mall? Aren't you tough enough? Aren't you man enough? I'm breaking up inside while I'm saying it, but I'm saying it because men get to work when they want and rest when they want, so you can't let them cry when they want or they'd get to do everything. So I ask him what he wants for breakfast, and, while he's eating it, I'm calling from the phone in the living room, and the line's busy, and then it's busy again, and then it isn't and I'm talking to Chris and I'm saying "Chris!" and she's saying "Ma!" and I'm breaking up in places I never knew I had. I'm noticing every breath as I take it, and I'm telling her, you think you know, baby, but you don't know. You don't know me. You don't know your father. We'll give you whatever help, whatever money, whatever anything. So stop crying, I say, but I'm crying when I say it, and Albie, he's crying no matter what I say. We're playing ping pong. I'm on the phone. He's on the phone. Me. Him. Me. Him. We're crying, and Chris is crying, and, after a while, there isn't any point, so we hang up and go to the kitchen and make a list. Number One: fix the phone. Number Two: fix the wall. I'm saying it, and Albie's writing it, and then we're seeing what he's writing so we're laughing, of course. We're saying we've got the kitchen to paint, so we might as well paint the dining room, so we might as well paint the living room too. The dining room's peach, and Albie loves it, and I hate it, and the living room's parchment, and guess what? I love it, and Albie hates it. Let bygones be bygones, he says. Paint the house anyway you want, he says. So we're looking at a sheet from Home Depot. It's got white, it's got pale white, bright white, off white, every kind of white. It's got a color that's kind of half-peach, half-parchment, and guess what? It's my sister. Now she's on the phone. She's like radar this one. She's like something the government should put on a satellite. She asks me, what's the matter? So I tell her about the paint, but she can hear it in my voice. You're crying about paint? she says. So I tell her the rest, and she's the oldest, so she tells me what to do. There's all kinds of retards, she says. There's bad retards and not so bad and there's retards you wouldn't know were retards if you didn't ask. These days they got retards doing everything, she says. My sister isn't Shakespeare but she's a good f-ing sister.

Excuse me. But you say what you have to say.

So I hang up and call Chris. I tell her, you and Kenny, go someplace, anyplace. Albie gives them fifty dollars, and they go to dinner or a movie. Maybe they stay home and spend the money on something else, I don't know. But we see them at church the next morning, and, one by one, people go over. They talk to Chris. They give her a hug, and they say a little something to Kenny, and you can see how much he's changed in just a day. It's nice. It's beautiful. Holy, that's the word. And guess what? The next day is Monday, so Albie goes to work. He's retired like we both are, but every Monday he goes to the shop to see if he can make a little trouble. He stays a few hours and comes home, and I'm doing what I always do. Nothing. Oh, I might read the paper. I might watch television. Anyway, he comes home and I'm watching *Judge Judy*. There's a guy with two wives, and the first wife is telling the judge and the second wife what a louse the guy was, how he never took her anyplace, and, when he did, he made her pay. Cheap date, I say. And Albie says, what do you mean cheap? And I say, I mean I'm watching the program and saying what the program says. But he says, you're saying fifty dollars was cheap, you're saying I should have given Chris and Kenny a hundred, well next time marry a Rockefeller. Doncha got a house? Doncha got food and clothes and that television? *Doncha!* He's saying the word like it's a swear word, and I'm saying it back, I'm making a face while I'm saying it, and he's saying I should do something to myself I won't repeat. I might as well do it since you can't do it anymore. Mother of God, forgive me for saying it, but I did, so he's yelling, and I'm yelling, and before you know it the kids are on the phone, Marie, my oldest, and Carmine, my youngest, and Lucille and Anthony, and Chris, of course. She's talking like Judge Judy. She's talking like Oprah Winfrey. She's talking like she's never had a problem in her life. Oh no, not her. Grow up! she says. Like we're not half in the grave already. And then I hang up and look, and there's Albie, he's going out the front door. It's ninety-five degrees, and he's got his coat on and his hat, and he's got his suitcase. He's leaving for the Y like he's always leaving for the Y. He'll never do it because according to him there's gays at the Y, as if they'd waste their time on Albie.

"Albie."

"What?"

"Get in here."

"Why?"

"I'm worried."

"So?"

"So, get in here," I say.

And when I tell him Chris is acting like nothing happened, he says, maybe it didn't. A - B - O - R - T - I - O - N, he's looking at me and saying this. And it's like peeing with somebody watching. I can spell, but I can't do it with somebody spelling right at me. I'm saying the letters, but it isn't helping, so I'm counting them on my fingers until I've made the letters into a word and I'm walking to the kitchen and there's the sheet on the kitchen table, the one from Home Depot. *Home Depot.* I say it like I discovered relativity. I say it like what I'm about to say had better work or we'll burn in hell, which we would by the way. Go there, I tell Albie. Go there with Chris so you can get the paint and she can get what she needs for the baby or tell you to forget it, she's not having the baby. You go, not me, because if she tells me, never mind the baby, I'll abort her. Kenny too, I say. So Albie picks her up. They drive to Home

Depot. They go to the Paint Department and tell the guy they want something between peach and parchment, and the guy pulls out a color, and it's the color of raw hamburger, I'm serious. And guess what? Albie wants to make the guy feel good. He's upset, and he wants to feel like he can make at least one person happy, so he buys the stuff. Nine gallons. Our house looks like it's been inspected by the United States Department of Agriculture. And they can't carry nine gallons, not the two of them. The guy gets a cart, and while they're pushing it to Kitchen and Bath, Albie does what Albie always does. He sees some batteries, he puts them in the cart. He sees an extension cord, that's right, in the cart. Two or three, why not? He's got masking tape, duct tape, four bottles of Crazy Glue, and a door knob. What's he want with a door knob? He's walking along having a fine time until he remembers and he's crying so bad Chris tells him to sit in a chair. It's one of those tables with four chairs and an umbrella in the middle of the table, and Albie's sitting in one chair, and Chris is sitting in another chair because she's pregnant, remember. Anyway, they're sitting, and Albie's crying, and one of the girls asks what's the matter, and Chris tells her, and she says there's a lady in Flooring who had a Down's kid. *Eileen in Flooring, extension 406, Eileen in Flooring,* she's saying this on the overhead. But Eileen isn't there. Somebody calls and says she isn't working that day but there's another guy. *Dave in Electrical, extension 406, Dave in Electrical,* this is blasting out all over the place. But a guy comes over. He's nice, I guess. He doesn't have a kid with Down's, he's got a nephew with a problem with his bones, but who cares? The girl sits with Chris, and the guy sits with Albie. They're sitting at the umbrella table like they're having margaritas. And guess what? The manager comes along. Get to work, he says. What the hell, he says. He's complaining until Chris tells him what's happening, and then he feels so bad he tells Albie to take the table and all the stuff in the cart and he helps tie the table to the car.

"What's that?" I say when they pull in.

"It's a table," says Albie.

"What's it for?"

"It's for sitting at."

And he shows me the chairs and the umbrella. He shows me the batteries and the doorknob. He shows me a step-stool. He tells me it's for standing on and reaching things. I know all about step-stools. *Did you ask her?* Ask me what? says Chris. And that's it. Chris is calling me a meddler, and I'm calling her a murderer, and Albie, he's walking around with the umbrella. He gets it off the car, and he opens it, and he can't get it closed. He looks like Mary Poppins. He looks like he might start singing or maybe dancing. And the Petraglias, they never miss a show. They're sitting on their porch, and they're watching until I walk across the street and tell Patty Petraglia to keep her dog out of my yard, I'll poison him if he keeps crapping there.

And guess what? Five months later, there's the baby. He's got the funny ears, the funny eyes, the funny fingers, and we're a mess all over again.

But guess what else?

Bing-bong! There's Patty with a lasagna. There's the Olneys with a pie. There are people we don't even know asking if they can do things. It's like I tell Albie, you don't know anything, Albie, not until it happens.

And *Albie*. We're married forty-two—what is it?—forty-three years, and Albie might have changed a light bulb. He might have opened a window if I told him I wouldn't get up and do it for him. He paints, but I have to get it all ready, I have to clean it up at the end. The only time Albie helps is when you wish he was doing something else, so I tell him, Albie, we've got a baby here, go in the basement and find something to keep you busy, which he does. He's down there a week, a couple of weeks. He's down there so long I get to wondering, what's he doing in the basement? Nothing, he says. What's he doing at Home Depot? I ask. Nothing, he says. But he's going there. He's buying stuff. He's got a list. It says two-by-fours, four-by-fours, this kind of nail, that kind of nail, every kind of nail. He's got enough stuff to build a house. He's got enough stuff to build every house on the street. What's he building? I ask. Noah's Ark, he says. But I know. It's the table, the one with the umbrella in the middle. Chris doesn't want it, and Albie doesn't want it, but he can't bring himself to throw it away. It's new, he says, it's nice. So that's what he's doing, he's making a deck to put it on. Once the weather breaks, he's out in the back working until one day he asks me to take a look. So I ask him, what's this? And when he tells me, I make like I don't believe him. Drop dead, I say. Drop dead yourself, he says. Well, maybe I will, I say. Well, someday, maybe we both will, so who cares? he says. So we get the table. We put it on the deck, and we get the margaritas. We sit there and drink until we're stupid, and, one of these days, we'll do it again. We'll do it with the Petraglias and the Olneys. We'll do it with Chris and Kenny, maybe, but not for a while, not until they're settled, not until the baby's settled and everybody's settled and life's not so f-ing crazy.

Excuse me. But you say what you have to say. And then you're done.

Mass Mental

Dr. William Welker was twenty minutes into a fifty-minute session with Kathleen Nichols when he found, to his surprise, that he wasn't listening. She'd presented with insomnia, which they'd decided was depression, which they'd decided was boredom, which they'd decided after a year and a half of once and sometimes twice weekly two-hundred-and-fifty-dollar therapeutic hours was actually a paralyzing fear of boring other people. Now they were exploring that fear. They were, one at a time, removing her defenses until she could sit before him and talk as she was talking that morning, if not the real Kathleen, as something close enough to evoke more interest than the usual Kathleen. Aside from killing the therapy, it would kill Kathleen to know that he too was bored. It would be like starting a surgery and walking away, leaving the patient to bleed to death on the operating table because he'd thought of something more interesting to do. Was it some resistance of hers? Was it some resistance of his, some resistance of his triggered by some resistance of hers that, once identified, would help him help her? Or was he just a lousy psychiatrist?

"Tell me, Kathleen. What does this conversation make you feel?"

"I don't know."

"What's the first word you think of?"

She closed her eyes. She opened them. "Uh-oh . . ."

"That's the word?"

"That's the word I think of when I think of the word." Then she said, "Prick."

"Say it like you mean it."

"Prick," she said again, exactly as she'd said it before. "How was that?"

"Fair enough," Bill wanted to say. Instead, he waved his hand at the skyline of Boston, visible from his window. "I don't see the sky falling down."

But it was. Or something was. Or it had fallen already because things went no better with Matt McNamara, his next patient. Matt was convinced that his wife of eleven years was having an affair, an accusation that his wife, juggling two children and a job because Matt had lost his job, repeatedly denied. "I wish," she said when he asked to see her cell phone log or credit card bill or followed her to work or, when he was really doing badly, from room to room around the house. Six sessions into what Bill had thought would be three sessions, four at the most, he'd told Matt that the man his wife was cheating with was Matt, the old Matt, the man Matt thought he could and still should be, only to have the delusions get worse instead of better. Eventually, they'd become violent, and Bill had called Mrs. McNamara as well as, at her suggestion, their West Roxbury priest. The threat of embarrassment before their conservative, working class community had kept Matt from acting on his feelings, which was good, but hadn't changed them, which was bad and—because of the expense—was creating a new set of bad feelings. So Bill was delighted when Matt said he'd had a dream. He was in a parking garage. He was there with his brother Hank, who was standing beside a '96 Toyota Corolla, telling him that there was something in the Corolla, something that Matt had to see. There was a man in the driver's seat, and Matt knew without looking that the man was dead and that he'd killed the man and that he was in trouble for doing so and then that the dead man was him. He both had killed the man and was the man. He was guilty of both murder and committing suicide, Hank told him, a feeling that explained Matt's self-destruction, although, that day, Bill couldn't say how. That day, he couldn't say anything, it seemed.

"This was in your garage?"

"A parking garage."

"Oh yes. You said that. I'm sorry. And you said it was your brother. That seems important. It was your brother Frank."

"Hank."

"The brother you don't like."

"That's Dave. Hank's the brother we go camping with."

"That's right."

But it wasn't. None of it was right, not with Kathleen or with Matt or with Al Davis, his impotent ex-Marine, or with Benjamin Marks, his cross-dressing bank executive, or with Phyllis Cunningham, his tranquilizer-addicted preschool teacher. Bill prided himself on liking, if not all his patients, some part of all of them, some part that helped him endure if not enjoy the other parts. That day, he found himself unable to endure anything about any of his patients until—halfway through his meeting with Martin Glass, a twenty-eight-year-old with what might or might not have been Asperger's syndrome—he realized what was happening and exclaimed.

"What happened?" Martin asked, startled.

"Nothing. I'm sorry. It isn't you."

It was Herb Bromley, Bill's chronically suicidal obsessive-compulsive. He'd cancelled that morning, leaving a thirty-minute gap between Charlotte Wurtheimer and Abigail Fredericks that Bill had used to check the messages on his answering machine. Three were from Herb, assuring Bill that he wasn't dead, his car battery was. "Get the joke?" he'd asked. There were two calls from patients wanting to change appointments and four from pharmacies reporting that one insurance company or another wouldn't pay for a medicine, and there was a call from an insurance company that wouldn't pay for a patient's therapy. There was a call from his wife, Cynthia, about the Schneiders. They were coming to dinner. Did he prefer Friday or Saturday? She'd called earlier, and he'd said Saturday, but she'd called Bev Schneider, and she'd wanted Friday, so now it was Friday or Saturday but they were discussing the Friday or Saturday of a different weekend. There was a call about his lawnmower and a call about lower than low mortgage rates from a bank in South Dakota, and there was a call from Jen VanDam, a therapist who was updating him on two of the half-dozen patients for which she did the therapy and he did the medication. There was a call from Deaconess Hospital about a patient seen in the Emergency Room and a call from Hebrew Rehabilitation Hospital about a patient he'd never heard of, and there was a call from Blue Cross about a survey they wanted him to take. Was he a satisfied Blue Cross provider?

And then, after the others, and seeming, at the time, less important than the others, there was another call. How had he forgotten? It was from Roxanne Wozniak.

"Hello, Bill. This is Roxanne. I'm sending you a couple. The Donaldsons. I think you'll like them."

———————

Bill did his training at Mass Mental, short for the Massachusetts Mental Health Center, when it was in its original building behind the Brigham and Women's Hospital. Built in 1912, it closed in 2003, its ceilings leaking, its basement flooding, its windows either not opening or not closing, whichever was worse given the season and the under or over performance of its ancient heating system. And the rats and the roaches and the ants and the mice and the fleas and the bed bugs and the scabies and the radon and the lead and the asbestos and the mold and the phones that didn't work and the exits that were locked because they led to fire escapes that had been removed and the emergency buttons that sounded alarms in a security office that was most often empty. The only guard the state budget allowed was out rounding or tending to other emergencies, and patient charts were stacked in the unused gymnasium as haphazardly as furniture was stacked in the unused swimming pool. If a patient appeared with any frequency, Bill and the other psychiatry residents copied the chart and put the copy in a cardboard box in the residents' on-call room in case the patient appeared and no one could find the actual chart. And good luck making the copy. From 1981, when Bill started, until 1985, when he graduated, you went to Suzanne, the secretary in the main office, and sympathized as she told you that her copier was broken or out of toner or making copies for some other secretary, you should use the copier in Linda's office, which, when Linda wasn't there, was locked, which meant that you had to talk to Bernie about the key, which meant that you had to talk to Georgina about the key because Bernie never had the key, which meant that you were getting close but, after getting the key from Georgina, you'd have to talk to Fatima, in supplies, about paper or to Franklin, in security, because Franklin, if he was working that day and he wasn't busy with an out-of-control patient, was the only person at Mass Mental with fingers long and thin but still strong enough to reach into Linda's copier when it jammed and get it un-jammed. And then, while you looked for Franklin, your pager would go off because the out-of-control patient Franklin was dealing with was yours. In the Day Unit. Or in the Overnight Unit. Or in Intake. Or in the middle of Longwood Avenue. Some days Bill thought that you couldn't design a system that worked so poorly if you asked a group of management professionals to sit down and do that specifically. But other days he thought that Mass Mental's inefficiencies were what made the place possible. The patients were so dysfunctional that having to interact with a half-dozen reasonably normal people several times a day to get a copy made or a prescription renewed—to do anything— was the only thing that kept the staff from going crazy. What would happen when he finished his training and went out on his own? Bill wondered until one day, he was out on his own and he stopped wondering because he knew. Without security, however imperfect, without a waiting room that would, however slowly, be cleaned if someone urinated on the carpet or smeared feces on the wall, Bill saw safer and safer patients until he'd moved from patients with big problems and no money to patients with no problems and big money.

"But what else can I do?" he thought when asked to see patients as sick as the patients he'd been trained to see.

The only connection Bill kept with Mass Mental, with the old Mass Mental, with Mass Mental before it was torn down and replaced with the new Mass Mental, was Roxanne. The Rox, the residents had called her. Beware of Falling Rox, they'd said after conferences at which she'd, once again, fallen. She'd arrive ten minutes late, so disheveled that visitors sometimes mistook her for a patient, and would seem not to listen. She'd busy herself with finding a seat and then with knitting or eating a snack or her lunch or staring at someone or something for so long that those who noticed would think that she couldn't possibly be paying attention. One of the residents would present a case, and there'd be a discussion, an animated back and forth between the residents and the attending physicians who supervised them and the psychologists and the social workers and the nurses who made up the rest of the staff until, as if on cue, Roxanne would raise her hand and say what everyone else had missed. "Was this patient born in another country?" she'd ask in her famous rasp, something like the sound of a shovel being dragged along pavement. "Did one or the other of this patient's parents abuse alcohol?" "Does this patient have a pet?" The presenter would look at her, as if to ask what a pet could have to do with threatening to throw your wife from a balcony or stripping at a City Council meeting until the presenter or one of the attendings would make the connection or enough of it that they would gasp or make some other gesture of understanding and the room would fall silent. I'll take mine on the Rox, the residents would say when they were stuck on a patient and decided to consult Roxanne even though, in rank, she was below them. She was a therapist. She'd received a certificate from the Boston Psychoanalytic Institute after two years of night courses and had come to Mass Mental before the state began to mandate minimal licensure. She'd been the victim of the quality-assurance initiative that had swept medicine in the 1990s and that had led to the building's closure in the early 2000s, and, when members of the resident classes from the 1970s and 1980s met for lunch or at the newly required continuing education conferences, the conversation would inevitably turn to Roxanne and what she was doing. She was just the sort of person the bean counters would get rid of, people said. She had the kind of ability you can't measure. She was a person, not a pie chart. Bill heard from Stephanie Tuke that Roxanne was working at Health Care for the Homeless and then, from Steve Marini, that she was working at a shelter for battered women in Worcester and then, from Pete Sanford, that she was, of all things, doing quality assurance. Left with no alternative, she'd joined the enemy. She was helping the bean counters make life hard for other unlicensed practitioners, people said, until Bill was at a meeting with Rich Keogh and Rich said that she'd started her own practice. "You're kidding!" Bill exclaimed, unable to imagine the Roxanne he knew running an office. Her talents were in the unconscious world below the apparent world. Her clinic at Mass Mental had run an hour late, sometimes more. Her desk had been piled with papers, and her chairs and the floor had been covered with shopping bags filled with more papers, and she'd sometimes smelled as if, like her patients, she'd spent the night in a shelter. The next time I hear about her, I'll hear that she's doing something else, Bill thought. But he didn't. He heard that she was doing well, that people were sending her patients. And then, he was too.

The first was Keith Whalen, a twenty-six-year-old office manager who'd presented with panic, which he and Keith had decided was an adjustment disorder, which they'd decided was a job that needed adjusting. They'd decided that Keith's job was below his potential and that his inability to succeed was due to adult attention deficit disorder or to an as yet undiagnosed reading disorder. To sort things out, Bill had sent him to Todd Snell, an expert in psychometric testing who'd called back the next day. "Just letting you know . . ." he'd said before telling Bill that Keith's scores suggested a major thought disorder and a tendency toward homicide. He hadn't seen scores like Keith's since doing his Ph.D. in the state prison system. "This guy could do anything," he'd said, upsetting Bill so terribly that he'd brought it up with Dan Sykes, the colleague with whom he met for a fifty-minute therapeutic hour of his own every week. Sometimes they discussed Bill. Sometimes they discussed Bill's patients. Sometimes they discussed Bill and his patients, their effect on him and his effect on them and the effect on the therapy he was giving them. When Bill told Dan about Keith, Dan told Bill that he didn't know about Keith, but he knew about Todd the Tester. He said that other practitioners had sent patients to Todd only to get a call about a seventy-five-item computer scored bubble sheet that proved, beyond question, that a man with a family and a job and an unblemished community record was actually an ax murderer. Dan told Bill to forget it, but Bill said that he couldn't, that he'd trained later than Dan and had more respect for the type of testing that Todd did, after which Dan suggested that Bill get a second opinion. He suggested that Bill pay another of his colleagues for a one-time, fifty-minute 'supervision,' a consultation just about Keith, which Bill did with Andy Thayer, who said that he didn't know Keith and he didn't know Dan and he didn't know Todd but he knew about lawsuits. "Dan isn't the one the family's going to sue when it turns out that Todd's testing was right," Andy said, which left Bill back where he'd started. He stalled his way through one session with Keith by telling Keith that Todd hadn't sent him his final report, which was true, and he stalled his way through a second session by saying that if he didn't get the report by their next session, he and Todd would communicate by phone, not mentioning that they'd done so already. Then Bill saw his patient Gary Halberstam, who was drinking again. "I'll take mine on the Rox," Bill thought as he listened to Gary, after which he looked up Roxanne's number.

"This is Bill Welker," he explained to her answering machine as well as who he was and why he was calling, and for days there was nothing. Then, one morning, the phone rang, and it was Roxanne, and she spoke as if they spoke every day.

"Did this guy go to summer camp?" she rasped after hearing the story.

Which, of course, he had. He'd been molested by a counselor at the camp, which had made him fear men as well as success as well as the tests that led to success. After ten sessions with Roxanne, Keith had retaken Todd's test and had scored normally, and Bill had sent her another patient and then another, and then she'd started to send patients to him. She sent him patients who needed medication and patients who wanted a male therapist and patients whose insurance wouldn't pay her but would pay him and patients who had agoraphobia, a particular interest of his. She sent him patients who met her and refused to see her because they thought she was weird, which she was—which she admitted she was—

and she sent him patients because she thought they'd be good for him. She'd sense something about the patient that seemed to align with something she sensed about him, some strength in him or some weakness or some mix of strength and weakness that would, in the course of therapy, prove useful to him. No therapy is successful unless the therapist too is changed. That's what he'd been taught at Mass Mental. That was the religion of the place. That was the beauty that had made up for the ugliness of the place. At some point a therapist, a real therapist, had to enter the therapy him- or herself, to plunge into the patient's perceptions and swim around before swimming back to shore and climbing out, wet and tired, but exhilarated by the experience of helping. The secret to caring for the patient is to care for the patient, to take a chance on the patient, to decide which patients are worth a chance and when and what chance to take. But why had Roxanne sent him the Donaldsons? Bill thought as Theodora Margolies discussed her fear of flying. And why had she said he would like them? he thought as Colleen Dempsy discussed her attraction to other women. Because he might not. What other explanation could there be? She'd sensed some trouble in the Donaldsons that would keep him from liking and maybe helping them until the trouble presented itself in therapy and he had either to face and overcome it or to let the therapy fail. That had happened with Ted Hartley, the African American dentist that Roxanne had referred for racism, there was no other way to put it, and no other way for Bill to treat Ted's racism against whites than to confront his own racism against blacks. That had happened with Anne Agostini, the repeated victim of domestic violence that Bill, too, had wanted to hit. That had happened with Pat Hogan, the substance abusing gym teacher that had reminded Bill of Mr. Terwilliger, the gym teacher who'd teased him for being chubby in fifth grade. Each of the patients Roxanne had sent him had been direct admissions to his deepest fears as a psychiatrist and as a person. Each had been a fastball, curve, slider, or breaking ball to one or another of his blind spots, the holes in his psyche that Dan and Andy and the other colleagues he saw for therapy or supervision tried but failed to fill because of the holes in their own psyches. When he told them about Roxanne and the cases she sent him and how difficult they were and how he initially retreated but then recognized and confronted one or another of his fears to his and his patients' benefit, his colleagues congratulated but also cautioned him. Don't romanticize Roxanne, they said. Beware of your oedipal issues, of our oedipal issues. She's the Madonna, the feminine totem at the center of psychiatry, the half-whore, half-mother we all want to sleep with and then kill because no matter how well we do our jobs, she won't save us. "Sure," Bill had always replied. "Thanks for reminding me," he'd said, even as he'd suspected them of wishing they had the courage to invite a Roxanne into their own professional lives. But why was she sending him a couple? he wondered. She'd never sent him one before. Couples therapy with a psychiatrist was expensive, generally too expensive for the people that found their way to Roxanne. Who are the Donaldsons? he wondered until, as Beth Humphries discussed the lymphoma that was killing her mother, he wondered out loud.

"I don't know," she said. "Who are they?"

Bill called Roxanne, but she didn't call him before the Donaldsons called. "This is Marie Donaldson," the message began. "I'm calling at the suggestion of Roxanne Wozniak who said that I should make an appointment, that we both should—I mean, my husband and me. She said that we should talk to you about—well, talking to you," the cheerful but quavering voice continued, leaving Bill confused. What was talking about talking? Did they want therapy or not? And who did she mean by "us?" Did she mean her and her husband, or was she referring, unconsciously, to another, more complicated, "us?" If she was like most women trying to drag their husbands into counseling, there were, at the moment, not one but two Maries, the Marie that loved her husband and the Marie that was starting to wonder about that love as he left her with responsibility for a marital problem he was willing, at most, to discuss the possibility of discussing. "I mean, we're doing fine," she said, convincing Bill that they weren't. "We just need a little clarity," she said, convincing Bill that more than a little was more than the two of them could handle. And the telltale word: just. As in, I'm just saying that we don't go out as much as we used to. As in, I'm just saying that we spend more time with your family than we do with mine. In Bill's experience, when someone used the word 'just,' the sentence that followed was a lie. And the self-interruptions! By the time she gave her name and her husband's name and their phone number and then said no, Bill shouldn't use that number, he should use her cell number, it was better than her husband's cell because her husband never answered and never checked his messages, she'd started and stopped fourteen times. Was it talking to a stranger that made her so nervous? Was it talking to the machine of a stranger, making a recording that the stranger could replay anywhere and anytime and to anyone? Or was it that the stranger was a psychiatrist and likely to do the sort of analysis that he was doing? No, Bill thought when he compared her discomfort to the discomfort he was used to causing people. This was more than discomfort. The part of her brain responsible for fight or flight was telling her to do both so forcefully that she was having trouble finishing a sentence.

And then, two days later, when Roxanne still hadn't called, Mrs. Donaldson left a message in which every statement was a question.

"Hello? This is Marie Donaldson? I called before, and I'm calling again to say that we'd like to talk to you? That we still do? If I don't hear anything, if *we* don't hear anything, today or in a few days—well, let's just say that we're waiting? So, if you could call me on my cell, I'd appreciate it? *We'd* appreciate it? So call us? Call me? This is Marie Donaldson, in case I didn't say that. . . ."

Bill pictured a middle-aged woman in an oversized house in the western suburbs or maybe an apartment in Back Bay. That would fit with the area code of the phone number that she had, in fact, left. He pictured someone white and upper or upper-middle class and either a professional or married to a professional. Why? Because in neither call had she acknowledged him. She'd acknowledged only herself and her expectations of him and her hurt and confusion when he'd failed to meet those expectations. She was used to control and lived in a house that reflected that control, a house sufficiently well appointed to command the respect of those similarly accustomed to control. Her house was so controlled and controlling, Bill thought, that her first awareness that there was a problem with the marriage had probably been a problem with the house, with the grout in the second-floor back bathroom or a persistent fog between the panes of the music room window. She'd wondered whether to call the company that had made the window or the contractor who'd installed it and had thought that it made no difference, that the manufacturer and the contractor were both men and not only incompetent but untrustworthy, like all men. No, wait a minute, she'd corrected herself: like all men except *my* man. That's why I married him, she'd thought until she'd mentioned the window at dinner, and he'd said he'd look at it, but he hadn't, not until she'd mentioned it again when they were going to bed the next night and again the night after that, by which time she'd noticed a stain in the ceiling of the play room and a gutter that had bent and a crack in the foundation of the carriage house they'd converted into a three-car garage. Left to deal not with a problem but with an ever-expanding list of problems, he'd said what he'd never said before. What the hell? he'd said. What is this? Call the window guy! Call the contractor! I don't care! She'd had either to confront his indifference to the house and, therefore, to her, or to swallow her anger and to call and organize a series of incompetent, untrustworthy, male contractors until, one day, while having lunch with a girlfriend, she'd let it all out. The house. The kids. The career she'd put off so that he could have his career. The changes she'd made so that, over five or ten or twenty-five years, he hadn't had to make any changes at all. And for what? So he could look at her and notice the changes and, instead of saying thank you, tell her that she was no longer the woman he'd married? So he could use one of his increasingly frequent business trips to have an affair unless she could find a therapist, a good one, which, thanks to her lunch guest, she did. There's this woman with an office at the back of a warehouse in Watertown. She's weird, but she's a genius. That's what people say. "But what happened then?" Bill wondered as he listened to the message for a second time. Had Mrs. Donaldson started with Roxanne and, at some point, decided that she and her husband needed to do couples work? Had the Donaldsons started with Roxanne and decided, with Roxanne's blessing, that they needed to work with someone else? And why, after deciding that he needed to know, from Roxanne, the answers to these questions and several more, did he pick up the phone and call, not Roxanne, but the Donaldsons?

"Hello," he said into their answering machine. "This is Bill Welker. Dr. Bill Welker. William, I mean. . . ."

———————————

Bill's first sexual intercourse was Saturday, May 16, 1975, at 11:34 P.M. He remembered the date because it was the date of his senior prom, and he remembered the time because it was immediately after the prom, while watching the clock in his father's big Buick Electra. In addition to a 455-cubic-inch, V-8 engine and the longest chassis and the widest wheel base of any car in General Motors history, the car had a dashboard clock with glow-in-the-dark hands that moved from 11:32 to 11:33 as Jessica Helmrath removed his shoes and his pants and his underpants and opened a condom and put it on him, after which he was in her, he had to be. He was sitting in the front passenger seat, and she was sitting on top of him, and he couldn't feel his latexed member to the right of her or to the left or when he felt around in the dress she held up behind her, so it had to be in her—really, positively, no-question-about-it-so-I-can-tell-all-the-guys *inside*—and it had to be there from 11:34 or 11:34 and a half until 11:38, which was pretty good unless the eight was a six, which he decided—over the next several days—it hadn't been. Having met each other at an East Greenbush meeting of the Albany, New York, chapter of Young Life, they'd spent a year-and-a-half interpreting the New Testament as needed to allow for necking and then petting and then—once in his father's Buick and once in her father's Oldsmobile—oral sex. And now this. The latest step in God's plan for their genitals. Rather than try again in the two weeks before he went to Africa to work with World Vision and she went to the Catskills to work at a summer camp, they'd decided to wait until September when he'd be at Amherst and she'd be at Holyoke and could see each other on weekends. "Better not to risk a 1 and 0 record," Bill said only to find on his return that she'd spent the summer having it off with a guy from Harrisburg, Pennsylvania. He'd been a cook at the camp, and it only made things worse when Jessica explained that the guy hadn't meant anything. He had a girlfriend doing a summer in Paris, and she had a boyfriend doing a summer in Kenya, and they'd both decided, why not?

"He taught me things that I can teach you," she said in their last conversation.

"Can he teach me to be honest? Can he teach me to be a Christian? Is this how Christians treat each other in—Harrisburg?"

Asked to acknowledge competitive feelings that he, as a Christian, couldn't have, Bill called Jessica a slut and broke up with her and went to Amherst and focused on his studies. He'd become a doctor. He'd work for World Vision. Night after night, he stayed in the library, studying chemistry, biology, and the other pre-med requirements until, one night, he opened the door to his dorm room and found Chelsea Reed, naked in his bed.

"What are you doing?"

"Waiting for you. I'm going to have sex with you."

"No, you're not."

"Yes, I am. You're going to take your clothes off—now, with me watching. You're getting excited just thinking about it."

"The only thing I'm getting is sick to my stomach."

"Prove it."

"I can't," he said when it was clear that he couldn't. "Please leave."

"Not a chance," she replied, getting out from under the sheets and sitting before him as casually as if they were sitting where they usually sat, in genetics lab.

"But if there's no God, there's no point," Bill said when they were finished and both of them were naked and sitting on the bed. "I mean, what's the point of saying that there is no point?"

"That's the point."

"What is?"

"That there is no good or evil beyond the good or evil we make for each other, so we have to make as much good as we can. That's why Sartre and Camus and the other Existentialists were the first to run off to South America or wherever else they were needed to protest the imprisonment of writers or other government injustice. And Beckett fought in the French Resistance. That's what *Waiting for Godot* is about."

"I thought it was about waiting for God to come."

"Sort of like waiting for a guy to come," she said giving his penis an affectionate poke. Over the two and a half years that they were together, Chelsea changed him from a born-again Christian to a born-again atheist, although he still wanted to be a doctor. He and Chelsea both wanted to be doctors in a small Vermont town where they could job-share a medical practice while farming in the summer and skiing in the winter, a vision that persisted when Bill did well in pre-med and Chelsea didn't. The feminist role reversal that had started their relationship was just that, they decided. It was a start, an idea to be used and then discarded as long-term couples have to use and discard many ideas. They'd go to Vermont, but he'd be the doctor and she'd plant what they decided would be not a farm but a large, organic garden and raise the children and maybe a goat and help at the children's school and give lessons at the local ski school, a plan that lasted until Bill went to the first of his medical school interviews and met women as pretty and as sexy as Chelsea who were going on to careers. Maybe they should rethink Vermont, he told her as he met more women at more interviews. Maybe he wanted to be a specialist. Maybe he wanted to be a surgeon. Maybe he wanted to be something you could be only in a big town or even a big city. Maybe he should go to Cleveland by himself, he said when he was accepted at Case Western Reserve. She could go to graduate school. She'd be graduating with a degree in Environmental Science, so she could take a year off and travel or volunteer for an environmental project and apply to a master's program for the next year. What would you do in Cleveland? he asked her until he was in Cleveland and she wasn't, an arrangement he finalized after meeting a classmate, a second-generation American Chinese whose father had swept the floor of a shop he'd eventually owned. Her name was Margaret Chu, and she was smarter than Bill, and she worked harder, so hard that she'd never had a boyfriend, which meant that Bill could do for her what Chelsea had done for him. She was better on exams, but he was better in bed, and he'd do better when they were out on the wards. She'd see what being a doctor was really about, he told himself until it was third year, and they were out on the wards, and, like most of the students who'd excelled in the first two years, Margaret continued to excel. She knew the answers on rounds and how to write orders and learned procedures so quickly and so well that she was allowed to do them alone. While Bill scored 'Pass,' Margaret scored 'Honors' on rotation after rotation until, by the end of third year, they were in different positions. They were training for different futures and had to decide whether or not to continue their training together. Unless they applied to residencies as a couple, they'd be placed in different residencies in different cities or even parts of the country. "So maybe we should see different people," she said before telling him that she already was. A second-year surgery resident. His name was Harrison. Harrison Something or Something Harrison, Bill couldn't remember because of Jessica and Harrisburg. Given the choice of staying in the apartment he and Margaret shared and having her leave him or having—in appearance, at least—him leave her, he decided to move in with two first-year students looking for a third, after which he got an honors grade for the first and last time.

"William has an unusual insight into emotional pain," said the evaluation for his psychiatry rotation. And Dr. Nethersole, the department chair, pulled him aside.

"I just want you to know," he said, "I think you're one of us."

"No thanks," thought Bill.

But internal medicine was too much micromanagement of chronic, generally self-inflicted illness in people so old they would die soon anyway. And pediatrics was fevers and colds except, once in a while, when the kids were seriously sick, which was terrifying. And he didn't have the hands for surgery or the nerve for obstetrics. Bill's interest in psychiatry was, in the end, an interest in the one residency he thought he could finish. It was an interest in one-in-twelve night call as a resident and a forty-hour week as an attending and an income better than attendings made in specialties that required sixty or eighty hours a week. It was an interest in having a life outside of medicine. And why not? Let Margaret work eighty hours a week! Let Chelsea do it! She'd changed course and was studying law and was engaged to another law student, a fact that bothered Bill until he applied to a half-dozen psychiatry residencies and got into Mass Mental and, the first day, met Natalie Messud.

"I'm sure it's here somewhere," she said as she walked around the Mass Mental parking lot, looking for her car.

"What kind of a car is it?"

"I don't know. I borrowed it from a friend, and I can't remember."

"Do you remember the color?"

"No."

"Do you remember if it was new or old?"

"New, I think. I remember thinking that it was very clean."

"Do you remember if it was a sedan or a van or a station wagon? Do you remember anything about the car?"

They walked around until Natalie said, "That's it!" after which she offered him a ride, which he accepted even though he had a car of his own. It was parked in the same lot, a fact he confessed later, after she'd confessed that she hadn't lost hers, she'd just pretended to in order to meet and start dating him. Her helplessness had been a pose, a signifier, the first in a series of ritual behaviors selected by human evolution to elicit a series of ritual behaviors from him until, over the next several months, they'd crossed or at least asymptotically approached the line at which people can be said to have coupled. As they learned to treat patients with varying combinations of Freud, Jung, Ericson, psychotropic medication, physical restraint, and — in the case of treatment-resistant depression—electroshock, they examined and reexamined themselves and the world in which they found themselves until Bill felt, for the first time, that he was in the world. He felt, for the first time, that he was in love, an arrival that made the other arrivals and departures of his life look like a stepwise and logical progression.

And then he met the Smiths. They met the Smiths.

"I've got a couples therapy in clinic," he told Natalie one morning as the two of them got dressed.

———————

The outpatient clinic was run by residents supervised by volunteer community attendings, and Bill's treatment of the Smiths was supervised by an analytically trained psychiatrist named Plotz. In addition to medical school and a psychiatry residency, Dr. Plotz had completed a seven-year, five-times-a-week psychoanalysis and would offer, Bill thought, an interesting perspective. Instead, he used their once-a-month meetings to forbid any perspective whatsoever. A therapist was to be objective with patients, to do and say nothing to interfere with their subconscious associations. It was a passive, classically Freudian approach that worked with Theresa Unger and Fred Behrens and Bernadette Thomas, Bill's other outpatient cases. But the Smiths were different. Bill's silence made them angry at Bill and at each other until, after a particularly tense meeting, Mr. Smith threatened to leave.

"This is stupid," he said.

So Bill discussed the Smiths with Dr. Ribikov-Youngman, the attending that supervised Natalie in the clinic. She'd written a book on couples therapy, and Bill read it and several other books and met with her and Phil Lamuraglia, the resident who saw Mr. Smith for individual therapy. Bill continued to meet with Dr. Plotz, but he discussed the Smiths with Natalie's attending and with Natalie until his relationship with Natalie and his relationship with the Smiths were inextricably linked. Mr. Smith had a part-time job in the primate lab at the Harvard Medical School and spent the rest of his time taking and retaking pre-med courses and the M.C.A.T. exam. Despite his poor grades, he was sure that he could be a doctor like the doctors he worked with and talked to at lunch and sat beside at lectures. They didn't seem so smart to him. They didn't talk about anything he couldn't talk about, and the lectures were never about anything he couldn't understand. But Mr. Smith was twenty-eight. He'd be thirty-five or older by the time he finished training. Mrs. Smith wanted children, and she wanted Mr. Smith to help with the children, and she wanted them to have benefits. She wanted Mr. Smith to work enough hours at the medical school to get Harvard's, famously generous, medical benefits, which meant that he'd have to make himself happy at the work he had rather than fantasize about some other, more exciting, work. She'd been involved with a would-be actor and a would-be musician, both of them remarkably like her would-be father as she called the alcoholic, perpetually unemployed boy-man who'd sponged off her mother. After a childhood spent parenting her parents, she'd involved herself with a series of men who'd needed parenting until she'd decided, after marrying Mr. Smith, that enough was enough. She brought him to Bill and told Bill to save them, which Bill and then Bill and Natalie tried to do. They talked about the Smiths over dinner and while driving the car and while lying in bed on the weekend mornings they both had off. Bill got up and got coffee and the newspaper and woke Natalie up, and they lay in the bed in Natalie's third-floor, Mission Hill apartment, looking down on Mass Mental as they fed each other oranges and read the paper and talked about the news in the paper and the news about each other and their colleagues and attendings and patients until the world they were in and the world they looked down on were both, in Bill's mind, the same. And the sex. It was so good that Bill wanted his patients to have the same sex, which was, as it happened, the sex that psychiatrists of that era were telling everyone to have. A woman could dress like Natalie, in heels and flattering outfits with jewelry and makeup, and still command professional respect, a post-feminist correction of gender relations that gave Bill and Natalie—at Mass Mental, at least—the status of pioneers. Their colleagues looked at them and wondered about them and listened when either of them spoke until Bill began to look at and wonder about himself. He began to listen to himself, as if struck, as if listening to some new and improved self until, one day, his new and improved self lost patience with the Smiths.

"We're getting nowhere," he said. "What do you guys want from this therapy?"

"To understand each other," said Mrs. Smith.

"To like each other," said Mr. Smith.

"You don't like each other now?"

"How can we?" said Mr. Smith. "She wants me to fail."

"I do not!"

"Are you sure?" Bill asked her. "Maybe you want him to be your father. Maybe you're afraid that a successful man won't need you." He told Mr. Smith to be manlier and Mrs. Smith to be more comfortable with a man, with a real man, and then he told Dr. Plotz.

"You've made a mistake!" said Plotz. "You're moving too fast!"

He was projecting his feelings of professional inadequacy onto Mr. Smith and was trying to save him rather than trying to save himself. His feelings were the normal feelings of any young doctor while Mr. Smith's hope to become a doctor was delusional and possibly schizoid and therefore dangerous to encourage. Rather than supporting Mr. Smith, Bill was making himself a competitor against whom Mr. Smith would fail, after which he might kill himself or Mrs. Smith or someone at work, an analysis that Bill reported to Natalie.

"Analysts think you're moving too fast if you're moving at all," she replied.

He should follow his gut. He should put Plotz and his five-times-a-week for seven years time frame out of his mind, which Bill did until, a few days later, he heard his name on the overhead speakers.

"Dr. Welker," said Charlotte, the switchboard operator who worked days. "Dr. William Welker. Call the operator. Dr. Welker."

Bill assumed that Charlotte was going to tell him that he'd blocked someone's car in the parking lot, which he had. So that everyone could fit, the staff blocked each other intentionally and then moved as needed to let each other out. "I'll be right down," Bill said when he picked up the nearest phone. But Charlotte said that he had an outside call.

"Dr. Welker?" a man asked when, after several tries, the call came through.

"That's me. Who's this?"

"This is Dr. Ephron in the Emergency Room at St. Elizabeth's. We've got a patient of yours. Derrick Smith."

"What happened?"

"I don't know. He's in four-point restraints, and he's screaming his head off."

"Is his wife there?"

"She's dead."

"Dead?"

"Killed by him, I guess. With a kitchen knife."

"How did you get my name?"

"That's what he's screaming. He says you told him to do it. He says you told him to be a man and let her have it. Have you got any beds?"

Bill called the resident in charge of the Overnight Unit, and he called Phil Lamuraglia, Mr. Smith's therapist, and Kirsty Allen, Mrs. Smith's therapist, and then he called Natalie. "You did nothing wrong," she said then and when the murder was reported in the paper the next morning and when, the next week, he was called before Dr. McCullough, Mass Mental's medical director, and Dr. Painter, the residency director, and Bernie Samuels, the adjuster that handled Mass Mental's malpractice insurance. Then Mr. and Mrs. Smith were presented at a conference at which there was a silence that even Roxanne couldn't fill. "Well, if no one else is going to say anything, I am!" Natalie exclaimed. "Bill told this guy to believe in himself. How can that be wrong?" Easy, said one attending and then another and then what seemed to Bill every attending in the room. Among the responsibilities of a psychiatrist is a responsibility to say only what a patient can safely hear. Among the responsibilities of a resident psychiatrist is a responsibility to follow the advice of his or her attending psychiatrist, in all cases, except a disagreement serious enough to be brought to Dr. McCullough or Dr. Painter. Bill had done nothing that was wrong but had failed to do a number of things that were right. They would have saved Mrs. Smith from death and Mr. Smith from a lifetime of incarceration and Mass Mental from the lawsuit the family of Mrs. Smith eventually filed. The suit named Bill and Phil and Dr. Plotz and Dr. Eric March, the community attending that supervised Phil in the clinic, as well as Dr. McCullough and Dr. Painter and Mass Mental and the State of Massachusetts. The suit asked for ten million dollars, reduced to two, and settled for one, which wasn't much, Bernie the insurance adjuster told Bill a week before Bill's residency ended.

"It could have been worse," Bernie said. "It could have been two. It could have been four. Not ten, but four—yeah. For this. It could have been."

"What's a seven-letter word for 'Hung up' that starts with C?"
"Careful?"
"With a Y at the end."
"Crucify."
"What's a six-letter word for 'Turning point'?"
"What's the first letter?"
"A."
"What's the last letter?"
"E. Or maybe two E's."
"I guess you have to kill me."
"I guess so. 'Four-time Cy Young winner, Greg.' "

"Maddux."

"Actor Alan in the movie *Popi*."

"Arkin."

"To disgust or to electrify twice."

"Apogee."

"What?"

"The turning point. It's the near point or the far point in an orbit. I can't remember, but it's one or the other."

After he and Natalie killed the Smiths and the Smiths killed them, Bill wanted someone outside of psychiatry and, if possible, outside of medicine. He wanted someone who taught second grade at the Heath Elementary School on Eliot Street in Brookline, which is what Cynthia was doing when Natalie took a job in Manhattan and he took a job close enough to the Heath to meet Cynthia jogging around the Brookline Reservoir. Odysseus had come home, not to kill the suitors in the hall, but to ask Penelope if she knew a six-letter word for impecunious that starts with *phi* and ends in *alpha* and the fourth letter is either *sigma* or *zed*. Romeo and Juliet had woken in the tomb, not to uncross their stars, but to spend the rest of their lives playing Scrabble with Friar Lawrence and Friar John. Although he and Cynthia faced their share of excitement having and providing for three happy and successful children, Bill took pride in how ordinary their lives were otherwise. It took, he thought, courage to be ordinary, a message he delivered to all his patients and had planned to deliver to the Donaldsons until Mrs. Donaldson made and broke three evening appointments. Bill required that patients keep appointments in his regular hours before he gave them an appointment in one of his few and much sought after evening hours. Canceling an evening appointment twice or no-showing once meant that a patient would be offered no more. He'd allowed the Donaldsons to start with an evening appointment and had allowed them to cancel an extra time because of their connection with Roxanne and because of the desperation in Mrs. Donaldson's voice, one that came, he was sure, from Mr. Donaldson's unwillingness to take time off from work. That day, Mrs. Donaldson had called and tried to break their fourth evening appointment, and Bill had said that they would keep the appointment or find another therapist, after which he'd had the most productive day he'd had in weeks. As if a spell had been lifted, as if no longer distracted by the siren voices of Mass Mental, he'd heard, for the first time, the anger Ron Samuels felt toward his mother and connected it to the worry he felt for his teenage daughter, one that was making his daughter act out sexually. He'd heard the ambivalence that drove Beth Humphries' careerism and the sadism that tied Theodora Margolies to her emotionally withholding sister, and he'd told Gary Halberstam to stop drinking. Bill had heard and said things he'd been trying to hear and say for months, and when he'd called Cynthia and heard about another of the crossword puzzles she left, half-finished, lying about the house, he'd wanted to weep.

"I love you," he said.

"I love you," Cynthia replied before saying that she'd keep his supper.

But what was this? Where were the Donaldsons? It was 8:00 and then 8:05 and then 8:10, and still they hadn't appeared, and Bill couldn't call them. Just as a stage needs a proscenium, a therapy needs a frame, an agreed upon distance that frees the patient and the therapist in ways they aren't by less structured arrangements. He'd have to wait until the Donaldsons called him, which, ten minutes later, Mr. Donaldson did.

"This is Lou Donaldson," he said with the assurance of a man used to giving orders. "Is this, ah—Dr. Welker?"

"It is."

"Well, I'm sorry, doctor, but we can't make it tonight. We'll have to reschedule."

"I'm afraid that won't be possible."

"You mean we should call back tomorrow, when your secretary's there . . ."

"I don't have a secretary, Mr. Donaldson. I make my own appointments, but as I explained to your wife, I won't be making one for you."

"Why not?"

"Because you've missed three already."

"So?"

"My evening appointments are for people who can't see me at any other time."

"Which is us."

"Which is a lot of people. Which is anyone who works during the day or has children to care for during the day or some other work or family obligation for which I'm willing to give up time with my family."

"Can I ask you something, doctor? You are a doctor, right?"

"That's right."

"A medical doctor?"

"That's right."

"Well, let me ask you something, doctor. What happened to doctors who make house calls? What happened to doctors who accommodate their patients?"

"You're under no obligation to find my services sufficient, Mr. Donaldson."

"I'm glad to hear that."

"You do have an obligation to tell me whether you want my services or not, so that, should you find them lacking, I can offer them to someone who doesn't."

"So, we're done?"

"Except for my fee."

"Fee?"

"For a no-show."

"You mean like fifteen bucks or something?"

"For appointments canceled with less than twenty-four hours' notice, I charge fifty percent of my usual fee."

"Which is?"

"Two-fifty. You owe me one twenty-five."

"Or what?"

"Or I'll put you in collection."

"You wouldn't dare."

"Actually, after three cancellations and a no-show, I would," said Bill, after which Mr. Donaldson paused.

"No problem, Welker," he said when he continued. "Whatever makes life easy for you. Good night."

"Good night," said Bill. And good luck, he thought as he hung up the phone.

Maybe they'd do better with the next therapist Roxanne sent them to. Maybe he'd loosened the top on the pickle jar just enough that the next person who tried would give a twist and it would come off easily. Maybe they no longer needed a therapist. Maybe having brought their issues to the surface, the Donaldsons could solve them on their own.

But as he turned from the phone and looked at the rest of the room, Bill noticed the chairs in the room, the chairs that would have held the Donaldsons and then the other chairs, the chairs he kept in three of the four corners in case he needed enough chairs to meet with a family. One was from Amherst, and one was from Cynthia's college, Wellesley, and one was a chair he hadn't used or really looked at for years. When word went out that the old Mass Mental would be demolished, otherwise law-abiding, state-licensed psychiatric professionals drove their expensive, late-model station wagons, vans, and SUVs to the back door and got Franklin or one of the other guards to open it for them and a spouse and maybe a couple of sheepish-looking teenaged children. From there they went through the offices and exam rooms or directly to the swimming pool in the basement and helped themselves to mementos they were sure the state wouldn't miss. Porcelain lamps and light fixtures and Arts and Crafts Era rolltop desks and exam tables and swivel chairs and just plain wooden office chairs built with pride in long-defunct American factories. The night he and Cynthia arrived in their late-model S.U.V., Cynthia charmed the guard into letting them in and helping them carry out the chair and two more that they used in their cottage on Cape Cod and an exam table that they used as a worktable in their basement. Now, Bill looked at the chair and saw, not Cynthia, or that night in Mass Mental, but Mr. and Mrs. Smith. He saw them in his office at Mass Mental, the one he'd shared with Yonatan Aladjem, the resident from Belarus, and Dale McAllister, the resident from Darling, Texas, which meant that, most days he'd had to move the Smiths to a different office because Yonatan or Dale or some other resident had been scheduled to see patients in the same office at the same time. He saw the khaki-colored ceramic tiles that were on all the Mass Mental walls and the battered brown linoleum on the floors and the banks of fluorescent lights that flickered and buzzed on the water-stained ceilings. And those big, wooden, straight-back chairs, the ones used in all the offices because, aside from being comfortable, they were easy to clean between the unbathed, incontinent, and sometimes vermin infested patients. Bill looked at the chair and saw Mr. and then Mrs. Smith sitting in the chair, and then they were sitting in the upholstered chairs in front of him. They were a construction, he told himself. They were the sensory product of an internal reality so vivid it was corrupting his external reality. He was having a trauma-related panic attack and should do what he'd tell his patients to do. Take a few deep breaths, he'd say. Say something. Shout something.

"We're getting nowhere," he imagined himself saying to the imaginary pair. "What do you guys want from this therapy?"

"To have my life back," said Mrs. Smith.

"To have my wife back," said Mr. Smith.

"Where is she now?"

"Forest Hills."

"Where are you?"

"Bridgewater State."

"Do you take medicine?"

"Yes."

"Does it help?"

"Only to remember."

"What do you remember about me?"

"That we were happy," said Mrs. Smith.

"That we were fine," said Mr. Smith.

"But you weren't," said Bill. "You were crazy. You both were. And I was a trainee. You have to forgive me."

Instead of responding, Mrs. Smith looked as she might have looked on the autopsy table, her skin drained of color, her chest full of wounds, fourteen Bill was told at the time. And Mr. Smith: Bill had pictured him as he'd been at their meetings, dressed for his work in the primate lab in lab scrubs. Now he saw him in prison scrubs, after which he had a more worrying thought. Mr. Smith might be out of prison. He might have been convicted of manslaughter and be wandering the streets of Boston, shuffling from shelter to shelter because of a past that kept him from having a job or a family or friends. He might have passed Mr. Smith on his way to work or to the symphony or to the art museum or to a ball game or out to an expensive dinner. "I didn't kill you," he said, this time out loud. "I don't care about you. Fuck you! Fuck both of you!" he shouted after which the Smiths were gone but another presence had taken their place. There was some depth to the silence that followed his outburst, some additional silence beyond the actual silence that made him think that he was sharing it with someone else. There was someone behind him, someone he couldn't see. There was someone standing in the door he'd left open for the Donaldsons, and his mind filled with embarrassing possibilities. Was it Henry, the janitor? Was it Chip Monaghan, the licensed social worker who sublet the office three evenings a week? Was it a patient of John Leventhal, the psychiatrist who saw patients no one else in the practice would? Bill worked in a four-office suite in a building with security in the lobby but none in the suite itself, and John saw patients he brought from his residency at the new Mass Mental, patients with dangerous, sometimes violent, pasts, and Bill wondered if one of them had come to find John and had found him instead.

"Is someone here?" he asked, turning his head slightly.

Worried that if he turned his head completely, whoever it was might be startled and leap at him, Bill turned his head a few degrees and then a few degrees more until, when he'd turned his head far enough, he saw a man and a woman, the woman a middle-aged former beauty who lived in an oversized house in the western suburbs, the man a middle-aged former high school or maybe college athlete who'd come from a job where the men wore conservative suits and spent the day giving orders. It was the Donaldsons, he knew. Like any couple in crisis, they'd decided to come and then had decided they wouldn't. They'd argued for a week before the first appointment and before the second and the third until, this week, they'd argued all the way to the parking lot and then had sat in their car and continued until they'd called and canceled and Bill had said to them what he'd wanted to say to the Smiths. He'd told them to go away, to leave him alone, to leave his memories of the Smiths alone, which, in the end, they'd been unable to do. As they'd started home, they'd thought about sitting alone, in opposite ends of what had, at one time, been their home, and had come back and parked the car and gotten out without saying another word. They'd reached for the other's hand and had hurried across the parking lot and into the building and now stood before him, fifty minutes late for a fifty-minute appointment, but ready, like Bill, to begin.

The
Woman
on the
Road

"Whenever there's three!" my mother would look at my sister and me and begin.

Whether three people or three countries or the Christians' Holy Trinity, I suppose, it was my mother's belief that two inevitably join forces against the third, assuring their individual as well as mutual destruction. The result, for her, was a steady stream of oddly contorted personal decisions, including her decision to have only two children, a strategy that might have worked if her brother Aaron and her sister Judy had played along. Instead they'd done what, in my mother's opinion, they'd always done: they'd conspired. How else to explain that Aaron had given his wife Liz, a woman whose name my mother had to stop and remember, not only three children, but three male children, three conspiring little Aarons, which freed Judy to have no children, no husband, no family at all? Aaron had her family for her while she played the doting aunt so wholeheartedly that What's-Her-Name? was pushed from the picture. That's what my otherwise intelligent, mentally balanced mother thought as she divided her time between Deborah and me and my father and working as a special education teacher for the Boston Public Schools. Each morning she'd grab what was left of the egalitarianism she'd nurtured through an undergraduate and two master's degrees and do what she could for kids crazed by the craziness of their families only to come home and be just as crazy herself.

My mother's response to the fact that, every year, Aunt Judy gave the five cousins birthday and Chanukah presents of precisely the same value and appropriateness: "You see!"

My mother's response to the fact that, every year, Aaron took his boys to watch football but took his nieces to watch baseball because we didn't like football: "You see!"

And so it was with the letters my great-uncle Lev wrote to my grandmother Ida during the five years he was interned at Stalag XVIIB, otherwise known as Lamsdorf.

My grandmother had left Lithuania and was living with my grandfather in New York when Lev, her brother, was drafted by the Polish army. Lev was forty-two and had a wife and two children, but it was 1939, and Germany was about to invade. When Germany won, the non-Jewish soldiers were put in labor camps while the Jewish soldiers were put in death camps or released to die in the ghettos, all but the Jewish soldiers who were Lithuanian. Considered Polish by Poland but independent by Lithuanians, Lithuania had never declared war, and Jews who could produce a Lithuanian birth certificate were allowed the relative privilege of incarceration. Before they too were killed, the Kehilla, the Jewish government of Vilna, found Lev's certificate and sent it to Lamsdorf where he was held for the duration.

The first *kriegsgefangenencarte* arrived April 22, 1940.

"Dear Ida," it said, in Polish. "I am writing you because I have written to Berta and the children in Vilna and have heard nothing. I hope that you are well and that you can tell me that they are well. Please tell them that I am well, and that I hope to hear from them soon. Your brother, Lev."

The next *kriegsgefangenencarte* arrived July 6, 1940.

"Dear Ida," it said. "Thank you for your reply and for the package. Because I signed for it and you got the receipt, you know that you can send me another package. Your brother, Lev."

He never mentioned his wife or his children again. He feared that the letters were being read and would be used to locate and kill them. And he was careful, in each letter, to thank his sister for the preceding letter and for the packages she sent through the Red Cross, reminding her and the guards who were reading the letters and stealing the packages that he had to be alive to sign for the packages so the guards should keep him alive. He even told my grandmother what the guards wanted.

"Dear Ida, I am well and hope that you are well. Please send me some shirts in a selection of sizes. And warm socks. I also appreciate personal items, like cigarettes. Your brother, Lev."

Thus cigarettes were sent to the nonsmoking Lev. And women's stockings so the guards could give them to their whores. And coffee. And chocolate. Even condoms. I don't know what they looked like in those days or how they were packaged, but I have no trouble imagining that, to keep her brother alive, my grandmother went to her Lower East Side pharmacy and told the startled pharmacist what she needed.

"Please," I imagine her saying. "As many as you have."

Out of the tens of thousands of Jewish soldiers taken by the Germans, a few hundred survived, and, thanks to my grandmother, my great uncle was among them. Tragically, his wife and children and his mother and father and all his other sisters and brothers and the rest of his community and friends in Vilna were killed, and, broken, he came to America and got a job at a bakery in Brooklyn. He'd been a mason in Vilna, but, after the war, my grandmother got him a passport and a job and an apartment he left only to work at the bakery and to have the occasional meal with my grandmother and grandfather. He never remarried, and he never mentioned the war or his family or his time at Lamsdorf until my grandmother died two years after my grandfather died and my mother was shutting down their apartment and found the letters and offered them to Lev, who told her to burn them, which she couldn't. She kept them in a box in our attic until Aaron wanted Steven, the oldest of his boys, to be bar mitzvahed, and the rabbi of Temple Beth Shalom in Passaic, New Jersey, refused. He said that Aaron had never attended much less belonged to the temple, so he couldn't have his boy bar mitzvahed in the temple unless Aaron and Liz became members and Steven did a mitzvah project, a condition that Aaron reported to my mother.

"So tell him to read the letters."

"What letters?"

"Lev's letters."

"They're in Polish."

"So tell him to read the letters with Lev. Tell him to ask what they say and where Lev was when he wrote them and what they make him remember."

"No!" said Lev when Aaron and Steven and the letters appeared at his apartment.

But Lev's boy had been Steven's age when he was taken to the ovens. The two of them were more than Lev could resist, and, over the course of several months, he read the letters, one at a time, and let himself, slowly, excruciatingly, remember them. He told Steven about leaving his wife and children. He told Steven about losing the war in eighteen days. He told Steven about arriving at the P.O.W. detention center in Radom, Poland, where the Jewish prisoners were separated from the non-Jewish prisoners and made to sleep in horse stalls that they were told to clean with their hands. And then, with the encouragement of the Germans, the Jewish prisoners were attacked by the non-Jewish prisoners. There was no heat, and the weather was cold, and, once they arrived at Lamsdorf, the non-Jews were told to take whatever coats and shoes and hats they wanted from men who only days before had been their comrades in arms. Lev told Steven this, and he told him about the guards stealing the packages he got from his sister, and he told him that while the Brits and Americans and Aussies and French were publishing a camp newspaper and entertaining each other with camp musicals and plays and, in one barrack, a jazz band, the Jews were living, all winter long, in open fields until one too many Brits were captured and the Germans went to the Jewish tent and asked for volunteers for a work assignment at Auschwitz. "Give us six men," the Jews were told, or however many the Germans could no longer accommodate, and the Jews had to produce them or the Germans would take them. Because of the packages, they never took Lev, a story that Steven used for his project. With the help of the temple, he reunited Lev's prison-mates, and Douglas, Aaron's second son, made it his mitzvah project to publish their recollections in a book, and David, Aaron's youngest son, made it his mitzvah project to get the temple to send the men to Israel with a stop in Vilna to lay a wreath at the site of the Kehilla.

Enough with Uncle Lev and the letters, I thought when it was time for my bat mitzvah.

We belonged to Temple Emanuel in Boston, and I proposed a report on Hannah Rachel Verbermacher, the Maiden of Ludmir, the only female rabbi in the history of Hassidism, but my mother would have none of it. She'd saved the letters and had given them to Aaron only to have Aaron get the benefit. All she got was Lev.

When Lev's landlord called Aaron because Lev was forgetting the rent, Aaron told Judy, and Judy told my mother, and my mother took care of it. When Lev's landlord called to complain about the mess in Lev's apartment and the complaints from other renters that he was walking around the building in his underwear, Aaron told Judy, and Judy told my mother, and my mother went down and cleaned the apartment and talked to the other renters and arranged for a nurse to come once and then twice a week until Lev fell and broke his hip and was in rehab for four months during which his apartment was rented to somebody else and my mother had either to find him a nursing home in New York or to find him one in Boston. When she found him one in Boston, she moved him up and visited him once a week and talked to him once a day, all to the objection of my aunt and uncle.

"You should have left him where he was," said Aaron.

"He was doing fine," said Judy.

And they threatened to sue when the nursing home, the Brookline Jewish Home, wanted to treat Lev for combativeness.

"I think my mitzvah project should be to stay out of this," I said, but my mother looked hurt. She looked as if, this time, Aaron and Judy had ganged up on her and I'd decided to join in. "I'm sorry,"

I said, which I was until she told me about Cat, a woman who'd pitched for the varsity softball team at Quinnipiac College.

When I failed to see the connection, my mother explained that Deborah was ten, which I knew, and that she liked to play softball, which I also knew, and that unless she got personal pitching instruction by age ten, eleven at the latest, she wouldn't be good enough for a college that considered sports in their admission decisions, a fact to which I confessed ignorance. From the beginning of March to the beginning of softball season in mid-April, my mother would drive from our home in Chestnut Hill to the nursing home in Brookline, where I would talk to Lev about the letters while she drove Deborah to her hour-long lesson in Natick and got back to Brookline before I'd exhausted Lev because Natick and Brookline were only minutes apart, a geography I doubted but knew better than to question.

"But isn't Uncle Lev confused?"

"That's only temporary," she replied, dismissing me in exactly the tone that Aaron and Judy had, on the same subject, dismissed her. "Lev will recover, and his doctors will stop his medicine and move him from the nursing home to assisted or even independent living and talking to you will speed the process along. It all fits perfectly," she said, and the next Tuesday, after driving me from our home to the nursing home, she said that she and my sister would be back in an hour when, including the lesson, it would be at least two.

"You must be Melanie Klein," said the woman at the reception desk.

"I must be," I replied, distracted by the fact that the glass, sliding door that had admitted me had done so with the sound of gas. "Where would I find Levi Rabinowich?"

"Room 436, but there's a problem." A problem? Had the floor been closed because of contagious disease? Had a water main broken or the building caught fire? "It's Tuesday afternoon, so he's in Activities," the woman continued, and I wondered if Lev and his fellow residents were out collecting litter along the highway.

But the woman told me to take the elevator to the second floor, where I found thirty or so of the oldest people I'd ever seen, some of them in wheelchairs, some of them seated in chairs at tables set with green napkins and cups and, at the center of each table, a plastic pot filled with what looked like Chanukah geld.

"You must be Melanie," said the woman in charge. "Lev, dear. Look who's here. It's your niece."

"Great-niece," I corrected her, although no one seemed to care or even to notice that I was there, including Lev. I made my way to his table and took the seat next to him, after which the woman continued.

"Can anyone tell me what day it is?" she asked, but no one knew or knew to look at the oversized calendar on the wall.

"Thursday?" someone said.

"Monday?" someone said.

"Thursday?" the first person said again. And then no one said anything.

"Actually, it's Tuesday," said the woman. "But it's a special Tuesday, and I want someone to tell me why."

"It's my birthday," said a third person.

"No."

"It's your birthday."

"No. But I wish it were. Think about what month it is."

"March," I said, unable to stand the silence.

"That's right, Melanie. Thank you for joining in. It's Tuesday, the seventeenth of March, and the tables are decorated with green, and what else do you see on the tables that might be a clue?"

"Geld," said a man with a tube that ran from a tank on his chair to a prong in his nose.

"And when do we see geld?"

"Chanukah," he coughed.

"When else?"

"The Olympics," said a man I'd thought was asleep.

"That's what the people in the Olympics like to see, or as they call it 'gold.' Who else likes to see gold?" the woman persisted, and when no one could answer, she pulled out a foil Leprechaun hat and pulled the thin, elastic strap under her chin. "Today is St. Patrick's Day," she said, looking around and smiling.

"How'd the pitching go, sis?" I asked when she and my mother came back as late as I'd thought they'd come back.

"Great," she said.

"How'd your time with Uncle Lev go?" asked my mother.

"Great," I said. "We talked about St. Patrick."

The next Tuesday I found the Activities Room on my own, but Lev wasn't there. He was in the auditorium, hearing a performance by students from the Brookline Music School. When I got to the door, a man was at the piano squinting alternately at the music on the piano and at a girl determined to make her violin play "Itsy Bitsy Spider" at a different speed than whatever speed the man played.

"Hi, Uncle Lev," I said when the man held the last note long enough for the girl to look up and stop and I was able to make my way through the other boys and girls and their parents to Lev and the residents he was sitting with. "Wasn't she good?"

"I thought she sucked," said the resident next to Lev, a fat woman holding a teddy bear.

"Well, everyone's entitled to an opinion," I replied as the girl's place was taken by a boy with a trumpet.

"That's not what they say here. Go here. Go there. Do whatever they say."

"I think we should be quiet."

"You sound like them. Are you a volunteer?"

"I'm Lev's great-niece."

"So?"

"So, I came to visit him."

"Lucky him," said the woman. "I don't have a niece."

"You don't have anybody," said the man sitting next to her who was holding hands with the woman sitting on the far side of him. The woman opened her mouth and wept with a high, continuous, sucking sound as the boy played a medley from *Star Wars* and I considered the corollary to my mother's rule of threes.

In any group of three siblings, whether three brothers or three sisters or any mix of brothers and sisters that totaled three, there's the smart one, the pretty one, and the 'other' one, the one destined to stumble through life, breaking his or her knees on plausible, easily describable self-identities the way one might stumble into sharp-edged furniture when crossing a patio in the dark. By having two rather than three children, my mother was hoping to get just the smart one and the pretty one. What she got was one who was both and one who was neither. While Deborah played softball and soccer and basketball and went to dance camp and took singing lessons and every other kind of lesson and made friends without trying or even noticing, my mother and father and the few others aware of my existence told me not to worry, my time would come. When? I wondered as I watched what seemed like everyone I knew lose themselves in wholesome, interesting activities that turned into an awkward hour of standing around, waiting for whatever it was to be over when I tried to participate. My sports were Envy, Irony, and Sarcasm, sports that were, in general, individual rather than team sports, except when one found oneself in a group of demented elders making catcalls at a nine-year-old belting out the theme from *Annie* like a four-foot-two Ethel Merman.

"What'd you learn today?" my mother asked when she and my sister came back.

"I learned that tomorrow is only a day away."

"Did Lev say that?"

"He sang it.

"He *sang* it?"

"That's right. This guy's playing the song on a piano on the stage and, all of a sudden, Uncle Lev gets up and throws his arms out and sings, 'Tomorrow! Tomorrow! I love ya! Tomorrow!' "

The next Tuesday, my mother called to be sure that Lev would be sitting in his room, which is where I found him.

"Hi, Uncle Lev."

It was the first time I'd ever seen him. Until then I'd seen him the way I'd seen the attractions in New York, of which, for me, he'd been one. There's the Empire State Building. There's the United Nations Building. There's the building where your grandmother lived when she was taking what her husband made as a haberdasher and what she made teaching a language she barely spoke herself to feed her and her husband and her three children and, every month, to send what was left to her brother. The few times I'd seen Lev, I'd seen what everybody saw, the broad face, the commanding brow, the inextinguishable fire in those all-knowing, all-suffering, but unblinking blue eyes. I'd never seen Lev like I'd never seen the lions that guard the New York Public Library. I'd seen them but I'd never sat in front of one and considered it. Now the lion sat before me, his eyes extinguished, his mane a few wisps of white rising from the back of his otherwise bald crown.

"I know you've told your story to my cousins," I began. "Are there any parts you forgot?"

Instead of answering, Lev looked at his roommate's empty bed, so I continued.

"What about your life before the war, when you were a mason in Vilna? What did a mason do in those days? Did you make walls? Did you only make brick walls or did you make any kind of wall?"

When that didn't work, I asked him about his wife and where he met her and about his children and where they went to school and where he'd gone to school, to grade school, and then high school and whether Jews in Vilna were allowed to go to any other kind of school, and, when that didn't work, I asked about Vilna.

"Was it big? Was it nice? Were the people nice?"

At last! After sitting in his wheelchair, motionless for ten minutes, Lev looked at me, his big, leonine head moving slightly ahead of his eyes until he gazed at me with either affection or loathing, I couldn't tell. All I knew was that I needed to know more about the only thing he'd responded to and that the only place I could do that was the place I already was. The home had a library that I passed every Tuesday, and, that Tuesday, after another ten unproductive minutes, I rolled Lev to the activities room and went to the library and found a row of books about the Holocaust, most of them about life before the Holocaust. There were books about pre-Holocaust Vienna and pre-Holocaust Danzig and Krakow and St. Petersburg and, just as I'd hoped, a book about Lithuania and one about Vilna. Built in the thirteenth century at the confluence of two navigable rivers, the city endured civil war in the fourteenth century to thrive as a commercial and cultural center until the wars between Poland and Russia in the seventeenth century, the plague and a series of fires in the eighteenth century, and the war between Napoleon and Russia in the nineteenth century. By the time Lev was there, at the start of the twentieth century, Vilna was known as the Jerusalem of Lithuania, a city famous for religious tolerance as well as the size and beauty of its Old Town, the largest in Europe, and for the parks, squares, lakes, and riverside esplanades that covered half the city's area.

I saw black-and-white photographs of couples sitting in sidewalk cafes and walking arm in arm along the rivers and families enjoying outdoor concerts and plays.

There was a picture of a boating race sponsored by the Maccabi Sports Union.

There was a picture of Jewish students sitting on a sun-dappled bench outside the University of Vilna. Seated from left to right were Rusia and her brother Abrasha Knysynsky, Rya Markon, and, behind on the right, Max Heller. There was another man, behind on the left, and it was my conclusion that he and Max were competing for the attention of Rusia and that Max looked relaxed because he thought he would win and that the man on the left looked miserable because he thought he would lose and because he couldn't live without his beloved Rusia, which she'd eventually figure out and make him the winner after all.

Except that she hadn't. They'd both been killed. Most likely, they'd all been killed.

And then I had to endure the fact that the people killed in the Holocaust included people who, at one time, had been as alive as I was alive, or I had to flip to the end, to the pictures of those same people lined up in those same sun-dappled squares until I came to a picture of a dozen well-dressed but unsmiling men and women, all in a row, with a row of well-dressed people sitting in front of them and realized that it wasn't a wedding or Shabbat dinner, that the people who were sitting were sitting on the ground and that, in front of them, was a trench filled with the bodies of well-dressed but unsmiling people who'd been shot as the sitting people were about to be shot and the standing people would be shot when it was their turn to sit.

"What did you learn today?" my mother asked when she and my sister came back.

"I learned that the Holocaust was a terrible thing."

"No kidding," said Deborah.

"Leave her alone," said my mother. "She's hearing Lev's story but hearing it from a feminist perspective. *That's my girl.*"

Who cared about softball? Who cared about my sister or my cousins or anybody?

And who cared if I was living a lie?

Every Tuesday, for the next three Tuesdays, my mother and

sister dropped me at the nursing home, and, after I said goodbye to them and said hello to Lev, I rolled Lev to whatever the day's activity was and went to the library and spread the letters on a table and tried to find what my cousins had missed. For example, from the first *kriegsgefangenencarte* to the last, there were forty-three, most of them from Stalag XVIIB but some of them from Stalag VIIIA, Stalag IVD, Stalag VIIIB, Stalag VIIID, and Stammlager 344. From the books I found in the library, I learned that each P.O.W. had been assigned a home site from which, when they weren't sent to Auschwitz, they were sent to build or to repair roads or train lines or to work on farms no longer sufficiently manned to keep the Third Reich fed. From each had come the same terrified lines. "Dear Ida, Thank you for your reply and for the package. . . ."

Maybe I could get Lev to tell me what roads he'd worked on. Maybe I could find them on a map and see if they were still being used.

Maybe my project could be to write to the German government and ask that Lev and the men he worked with receive reparation for the roads they'd built and the train lines they'd repaired, or maybe I could get Lev to describe what the cousins had touched only briefly, the selection of Jews by their fellow Jews for transfer to Auschwitz.

In his report, Steven said that the Jews had decided among themselves, choosing the oldest and most infirm to go. But who'd decided that? I wondered as I reflected on the comparatively easy task of deciding which of my friends would and wouldn't be invited to my bat mitzvah.

I was wrestling with the fact that Beth Lieber had made friends with Laura Gund after being in a play with her and that Beth had told Laura that my friend Emily Hauser had a crush on Adam Berg, which Laura had told Adam, which had made Adam stop talking to Emily, which had made Emily stop talking to me because she thought that I'd told Adam, which I hadn't, a fact that I'd explained to Beth in such a way that it had sounded to Beth as if I were accusing her of spoiling my friendships with Emily and Adam, which I was. Now I had to decide whether I was going to invite Beth to my bat mitzvah and have Emily not come or whether I was going to invite Emily and have Beth not come or whether I was going to invite all of them and invite Adam, which would make all of them come whether they wanted to or not because everyone, including me, had a crush on Adam. What would it have been like to look Beth or Laura or Emily in the eye and say, "Sorry Em, but the Nazis have asked for a twelve-year-old Jewish girl and the rest of us have noticed that you've been looking a little tired. Just sayin'."

Is that why Lev had never talked about the Holocaust, because he'd survived when so many hadn't? And what about the gap from the last *kriegsgefangenencarte* on June 15, 1944, and the letter he wrote from a displaced persons camp on April 30, 1945?

In his report, Douglas said that the letters took weeks at the start of the war but months at the end and then stopped altogether because, as the Russians advanced, the prisoners were moved to build battlements, making delivery impossible. Finally, the Germans used the prisoners as hostages, keeping them from Russian hands in order to gain leverage in the increasingly likely surrender talks. On February 20, 1945, the prisoners were marched, half-starved and poorly clad, from East Germany to West Germany, a five-hundred-mile ordeal about which the prisoners differed. One reported that the non-Jews were guarded by a company of German infantry while the few remaining Jews were guarded by a ragtag of Yugoslavians told to shoot anyone who complained or got frostbite or couldn't march for weeks without rations, but another prisoner said no. He described the guards as friendlier as the march went along until, one day, they broke off from the rest of the column and hid the Jews in the woods. Hoping to be identified as Yugoslavian rather than German just as, at the beginning of the war, Lev had been identified as Lithuanian rather than Polish, the Yugoslavians marched the Jews by day and hid them by night until they were discovered by a Russian patrol, a point in the story at which the recollections differ again. One prisoner said that the Russians and the Yugoslavians killed each other and most of the other prisoners, but another remembered that the Russians snuck up and executed the still-sleeping Yugoslavians and told the prisoners to run. "If we capture you, we'll take you to Russia and you'll be put in a camp worse than the one you just came from," the Russians said in that version while in another they said, "You'll slow us down and get us killed, so hurry up and beat it out of here before we change our minds." The only thing on which the prisoners agreed was that, after leaving the forest and reaching a road, they met a woman on the road, another prisoner freed from another prison or death camp, a woman with no hair and no clothes other than the smock the Germans had given her. "You're safe with us," the men told her after which they went door to door and got her clothes.

And then the prisoners are saved and Lev and the woman are saying goodbye and promising to write, which, for several years, they do.

Who was she? I wondered in the way I wondered if Adam Berg and I would get married because, after the trouble with Emily, he'd said hello to me twice in one week. I knew that we wouldn't the way I knew that Lev hadn't fallen in love with the woman— that Lev, as far as he could have known was still married—which is to say that I both knew it and didn't. I was hearing Lev's story, not from a feminist perspective, but from a child's perspective, but was too much a child to know the difference.

"I think that sis and I should come in with you and thank Uncle Lev," my mother said as we drove to my sixth and final Tuesday.

"If you don't mind, I'd like to thank him myself."

That's my girl. My mother didn't say it, but she gave me a look that said it, and Deborah gave me a look that said that she'd noticed.

"Hi, Uncle Lev," I said before rolling him not to the activities room but to the solarium at the end of his hall. The home was on a ridge and the solarium looked over the grounds of the home and the skyline of Boston, which suited my plan.

"That's Boston," I said. "Did Vilna look like Boston? Did it look like New York?"

Nothing.

"I read in a book downstairs that there were parks and rivers, and there was a picture of some races on a river. Did you ever see those? Did ever you race in those?"

Nothing.

"Did you ever hear of the Maccabi Sports Union?"

Nothing. It was time to make my move.

"I read in another book that you and the other prisoners were marched through two feet of snow without boots or hats or gloves or food or even places to stay. Townspeople were shot if they helped you, and sometimes the guards were nice and sometimes the guards shot you with no explanation. And then you're hiding in the woods and some Russians find you and shoot the guards and tell you to go west, which you do, but by then it's March or even April, so the snow must be gone, and the sun must be out, and the fields must be full of flowers and the streams must be flowing with water you could bend down and drink. It must have been beautiful. After all that time in the prison camp, it must have seemed like heaven. And then, one day, you're walking along and you meet a woman."

As I waited for Lev to respond, a pair of nurses walked past the door. They were speaking a foreign language, Haitian I remember, although at that age I wouldn't have known the difference between Haitian and an African language or even heavily accented Spanish or Portuguese. They said what they were saying and then laughed and were gone, and I asked my question again.

"She must have been somebody special if you went to peoples' doors and asked them to give you clothes without knowing if the people would help you or shoot you or call the Nazis and have them shoot you. Who was she?" I asked, and again the big, leonine head turned, the head moving slightly ahead of the eyes until his eyes were fixed on mine, but this time he leaned forward. The nurses had belted him before allowing me to take him, and he leaned as far as his belt would allow and spoke so softly that I leaned forward as well, turning one ear so I wouldn't miss a word.

"She was a Jew!" he whispered, his breath a sickening mix of medication, vanilla- or maybe strawberry-flavored food supplements, failing health, and the faint smell of excrement that was so pervasive at the home I smelled it for days after each visit. "The Germans should have killed her! They should have killed all of us!" he hissed, his eyes narrowing and looking no longer at me but through me, at something deep, down, at the center of me until, satisfied that he'd seen it, he looked away, his big head again moving ahead of his eyes until he leaned back and looked out the window as blankly as the other residents who were sitting with their families.

Had he seen through my plan? Was he mocking me? Or had he seen something else, some suffering at the center of me that had made him, for a moment, trust me with the suffering at the center of him?

Or was he, as the nursing home said, intermittently incoherent?

"How'd it go?" asked my mother when she and my sister came back from my sister's last session with Cat.

"Great," I said. "He told me a story that he's never told anyone."

"Can you use it for your project?"

"Now that you mention it, yes. I think I can," I replied, deciding to tell my mother and my rabbi that I'd looked for and found the woman on the road when, in fact, my mitzvah would be a second flooding of the earth. After my twice-weekly Hebrew lessons, I scoured the Torah for anything that my mother would find offensive—references to incest and the rape of female prisoners and the selling of daughters into slavery and the prohibitions against women making contracts or having extramarital sex, a sin for which they but not men were killed—all of it leading to a finale that included my mother's drinking and my father's year and a half of unemployment. And the rule of threes, you bet. And the corollary. And what Uncle Lev had said, what my mother and her competition with her brother and sister had made him say, I thought as I sat in Temple Emanuel, the speech in the right pocket of the Annie Hall–style, oversized sweater I'd chosen not because it was the 1980s and that's what twelve-year-old girls wore but because it had two such pockets, one pocket for the speech I would pull out if anyone asked to see it, the other pocket for the speech I would pull out after Steven had opened the ark, and Dafna Herzel, the daughter of friends of my mother and grandfather, had walked the Torah around the sanctuary, and Aaron and Liz had read the first aliya, and Dafna and her husband and their children had read the second, and my mother's roommate at Vassar had read the third, and a friend of my father's from law school had read the fourth, and Judy and Douglas and David had read the fifth, and my mother and father and Deborah had read the sixth, and the Kriegers and the Snitzers, two families from Rashi, the Jewish day school my sister and I attended, had read the first and second halves of the seventh, respectively, and Shefa Lidman, the rabbi, had invited me to the Torah and smiled when I'd chanted, without flaw, the maftir, which was from Genesis. Then Rabbi Lidman, known to the Emanuel kids as 'Shuffling' Lidman, shuffled to one side, and I spread the speech on the lectern.

"Mazel tov!" I thought as I looked at those who'd read and at the rest of them, the other families in the temple and Beth and Laura and Emily and Adam and the rest of my friends until, at the last moment, I saw Lev.

He was in the aisle, sitting in his wheelchair, and I almost missed him because I kept looking at Adam who was across the aisle and because Lev was dressed in a way I'd never seen him dressed before. He was dressed like the people in the picture, the one of the people waiting to be shot, a picture that I suddenly understood. Rather than go to each house, chasing the Jews who'd heard shooting at the first house and had grabbed their families and run or, even less convenient, had grabbed guns and were firing back, the Germans had waited until Saturday and surrounded the temple. That's why the people in the picture were dressed the way they were. They were dressed for services. They were dressed the way Lev still dressed for services.

"For those of you who don't speak Hebrew, the passage I read was about Kashrut, the dietary law, and I wrote a speech about refusing to eat everything so we can take pleasure in eating a few things and thereby find the freedom that comes from accepting confinement. My speech said that there is a similar freedom to be found in the confinements of marriage and parenthood, and I thanked my parents and my uncle and my aunt and my great-uncle Lev who spent six Tuesday afternoons with me. I learned about his confinement at Stalag XVIIB, otherwise known as Lamsdorf, and I wrote a speech that I could read and that you'd like except that I'm not going to read it. Instead, I'm going to read a different speech, a new speech," I said. But when I looked at the paper, I couldn't see the words. "A speech about . . . the woman on the road," I continued, reading not my sham speech or my real speech but making one up, using parts of both as I went along. "During my Tuesdays with Uncle Lev, I heard that story, but this time I heard it differently. I heard it from a feminist perspective as my mother likes to say. What would it be like to be a woman walking along a road with Russian and German and Yugoslavian and American and British soldiers all around, and there you are, by yourself, and you see a dozen men coming down the road, right at you? What would it be like to be a Jewish woman and find out that the men were Jewish men? I don't think you'd be thinking about the stuff that makes feminists so crazy when they read it in the Torah, the stuff about selling us into slavery and not letting us sign contracts and all the stuff about stoning us and burning us. I bet she was thinking, Hey, what do you know? These guys are Jews. I'm O.K. And she was. And so am I." I said that to be bat mitzvahed is to become a Jewish woman and to be a Jewish woman is to know that there are Jewish men, men who made mistakes but took the time to write them down and think about them so they could do things better the next time. "Which is all you can ask of anybody," I said, and, when I looked, I saw, to my amazement, that no one was upset. They looked as if I'd said what every kid says, in one form or another, at every bar or bat mitzvah. Somebody yelled Yishar Koach, and somebody threw candy, and Uncle Aaron and Aunt Judy and everybody else in the family looked happy with me and, for once, with each other, including my mother, who, if she knew what had happened, said nothing until, two years later, when she threw dirt on Uncle Lev's coffin.

"We didn't save you," she said. "You saved us."

Fergus B. Fergus

The Olneys had two cats: an old, gray female named Smoke and a younger cat, the product of her one and only litter, an amiable, tiger-striped male named Fergus. Fergus B. Fergus, the Olney kids called him although, when Dan asked, no one knew why or what the B might stand for. They acted as if the cats, like the rest of their lives, were slightly beyond Dan until, one Christmas, Mrs. Olney asked Dan if he'd take care of the cats. The family would be skiing in Vermont and would pay him three dollars a day for nine days, a lot of money for 1965 and a *real* lot for a boy who was ten. Then school was out, and the Olneys drove away, and Dan looked down the row of suburban tract houses from his house to their house with a sense of possession. The color became his, Pilgrim Blue, a touch of the Olneys' New England heritage. The trees became his, the trees in the front, the ash big enough to climb although Dan never had, and the evergreens, enough of them in a bunch to use as a hideout although Mr. Olney forbade it. Even the square painted on the garage door, a target for Todd Olney, who was older, and A. J., who was Dan's age, and Lauren, who was younger, to work on their backhands.

And how peaceful it looked. How still and dignified compared to his own house now that he had to spend all day with his younger brothers Tom and Andy.

With his father at work, it was them and his mother and their dog, a poorly trained rescue named Bud. Bud barked and cowered, with no apparent pattern, and he chased cars and sometimes bikes, and he smelled bad and shed and wet the furniture and carpets. One result of Dan's newly recognized capacity to care for the Olney pets was an insistence by his father that Bud be cared for, that Dan feed him and walk him and brush him and do his best to train him. For weeks, Dan had anticipated the Christmas break only to have it arrive and feel that he was trapped by the dog, by his brothers and their whining that there was nothing to do, by his mother and her warnings that the three of them had better find *something* to do, which they couldn't because, whatever it was, they would have done it with the Olneys.

"No," said Dan when Tom asked if he could help with the cats.

So there was no turning back, no asking his brother or his mother to join him when, that night, he went outside and found that it was darker than he'd expected. The only light was the light that spilled from the windows of every house but the house he was, for some reason, walking toward, its blue brooding and black, its windows even blacker, the branches of the ash raised as if to stop him from continuing up the tracks the Olneys' station wagon had left in the snow on their driveway. Then he got to their front step and something leapt at him. "Fergus!" he exclaimed before opening the storm door and unlocking and opening the main door, after which he followed Fergus inside, turning on lights until he'd reached the kitchen in the back and turned on the light for the kitchen porch. From the back yard, Smoke appeared, and he let her in and put food for her and Fergus in bowls on the kitchen floor and left, turning the same lights off, in the same order, until he was back in his boots and going out the front door, reaching in to turn the last light off before closing the door and locking it and hurrying back to the street.

"How did it go?" his mother asked when dinner was ready.

"How did what go?"

"Taking care of the cats."

"O.K.," Dan replied, still too upset to eat.

But in the morning, in the full light of day, he walked over and let himself in and spoke with confidence.

"Well, guys, anything to report? Any strangers around this morning?"

He went to the living room and sat on the couch until, after a few minutes, Smoke came and sat beside him and Fergus came and sprawled across his lap. "Just give the feeling that someone's home," Mrs. Olney had instructed, so Dan sat like that for an hour, relaxing in a way he never had in the Olneys' house or even his own. He'd never been alone, not for long, and he was experiencing the first, heady pleasures of solitude. He could do anything, say anything, and no one would know, although, at that moment, he was too conscious of the Olneys to do very much. He imagined them there in the living room, watching as he stroked Fergus on the ears, on the chin, on the chest so expertly that Fergus purred himself into a paralysis of rumbling pleasure. He did the same to Smoke and, after, put them both outside, and he did the same the next morning, and the next, each time making a hurried, heart-pounding visit at night but, to compensate, a more professional visit the next day. Always careful to get up and head over before his brothers were up, he'd walk over and let himself in and sit in the silent house until he was spending less time imagining the Olneys and more time imagining what he'd imagined about the house's outside, that its inside, too, was his: the couch he sat on, the coffee table he was eventually comfortable enough to put his feet on, the Olneys' antique furniture and the books they had on the living room shelves and the grandfather clock whose slow, resonant tick distracted him from the house's occasional creaks and groans. Eventually, he was comfortable enough to walk around on his visits, to the den, to the playroom in the basement, and to the upstairs bedrooms—A. J.'s, which he'd been in before, but also Todd's and Lauren's—not touching or even looking at anything, just standing there savoring the feeling that he shouldn't be until one day he found himself savoring a Sara Lee Traditional Recipe All Butter Pound Cake.

It was in the refrigerator, and every day, when he'd given the cats milk, he'd seen the cake and had lifted the lid and had seen, once again, that half of it was left and had thought about finding a knife and slicing a piece too thin to be noticed. Maybe it was the fact that the cake was getting stale there in the dry and the cold and that, in all likelihood, the Olneys had forgotten it in the hurry of packing and would throw it out on their return. Maybe it was the fact that, by that day, the fifth of the nine he'd be working for the Olneys, their departure was as distant as their return, and they'd faded from his mind as far as they would that vacation. Maybe it was the fact that it was the day after the day after Christmas, and he was feeling empty. He wasn't hungry, not for anything he could eat, not for more sweets, given the holiday and all he'd eaten already and could still eat at home. Whatever the explanation, he saw the cake, and, in a second, a knife was in his hand, and a piece was cut, and another, and, still wondering what he'd done, he washed the yellow, crusted frosting from his hand and from the knife and dried the knife and returned it to its drawer and searched the cupboards for something else he could plunder. He found a bag of cookies that was open and full enough that no one would notice the loss of one or two, and he found a jar of cashews that was open and some M&Ms, and, when he looked in the freezer, he found a container of chocolate swirl ice cream with a hollow in the center that he widened by several swipes of a spoon that he also washed and dried and put away.

And then he saw the nudes, Mrs. Olney's nudes, the six-inch statues she made at various times in her various art classes and left around the house.

There was one on the bookshelves in the living room and one on the shelves in the den and one on the piano and two on the lowboy in the dining room. Dan had seen them before, when the Olneys were there; anyone could. Todd had explained that she'd made them in a class where a lady had sat naked in front of everyone. He'd waited for Dan's reaction, and Dan had known better than to have one and had kept his glances at the statues brief or hadn't looked at them at all. But that morning he looked at the nudes on the lowboy and noticed their faces, less than expertly rendered but faces nonetheless, one of them smiling, the other looking as if she was perfectly happy to let a whole bunch of strangers stare at every part of her for as long as they wanted. With his heart pounding as it had when he'd made his visits at night, Dan went over to the nude that was smiling and looked at her breasts and then at her nipples, wondering at the fact that Mrs. Olney had made the breasts and then two little dots of clay and had attached them to the breasts, looking from the woman to her statue and back again to be sure the breasts were right and then that the nipples were right, maybe even taking the nipples on and off until she got them just right. Then he looked between the statue's legs, not sure what he was looking for, not sure what was between a woman's legs, but the smiling nude's legs were closed and the other nude's legs were apart but the details had been left unfinished, and, ashamed but unable to control himself, he turned from the nudes on the lowboy and went to the other nudes, the one in the den and the one on the piano and the one on the shelves in the living room. In each case, he looked at the breasts, at the buttocks and pelvis, struggling to imagine whatever details Mrs. Olney hadn't chosen to provide.

And the faces, those untroubled faces.

They were faces like the faces of women he knew, not his mother, certainly, but Mrs. Olney and the other women who lived on Royal Crescent, Mrs. Spector and Mrs. Johnson and Mrs. Green and Mrs. Petraglia and Mrs. Kennard. They were faces like the women at church or the mothers of the kids at school or the boys on his swim team at the Y or the women who taught him at school, Mrs. Johnson or Mrs. Tuke or, his social studies teacher, Miss Byrne. In social studies, they were studying Greece, and, right before school was out, she'd shown the class a picture from a tall, glossy book. It was a painting of acrobats in Crete bull-jumping, grabbing a charging bull by the horns and vaulting themselves up and over it, which was interesting, but nowhere near as interesting as a woman in the painting who was topless.

"There's no reason to laugh," Miss Byrne had said when several boys had done so. "Different cultures have different ideas about privacy," she'd continued, and Dan had been grateful that he hadn't laughed.

But now, in the privacy of the Olney house, in the privacy of his morning of sin, another sin began to form in his mind. He wondered if Mrs. Olney had any books, any tall, glossy books with similar paintings, and, stepping back from the shelf, he looked at the other shelves. There was a shelf for *The World Book*, their encyclopedia, and a shelf for an ancient *Britannica* from Mr. Olney's childhood, one he and A. J. sometimes looked at to laugh at the pictures of old-fashioned airplanes and cars and cameras and trains and the maps that, with the passage of time, had countries with outdated borders and names. There was a shelf of bird watching books and a shelf of books about antiques and a shelf of books about fishing. There was the Olneys' stereo system, a turntable and amplifier and two speakers, up where small children couldn't reach them and, up, above that, a shelf filled with stuff Mrs. Olney had inherited from a relative who was a sea captain, a compass and a spyglass and a mask from some South Sea island, and, up, above that (so high that Dan had to pull an old wingback over so he could stand on it and reach up while standing on his toes), a shelf of the sort of books he was looking for.

Gently, he took the first, holding it with one hand as he used the other to carefully turn each page. *The Paris I Love*, the book was called. There were pictures of the *Folies-Bergère*, and there were pictures of people on a beach, and there were some time-lapse pictures of famous sites that showed all the traffic going around the sites at night with their headlights and taillights fused, an effect that Dan had never seen and which he liked, but there was nothing like the pictures Miss Byrne had shown. He put the book back and took another, one about Rome, a good bet, he thought, but it, too, was a travel book. It had nice but uninteresting pictures of other famous sites, as did another book, one about California, and he was about to give up when he saw a book called *Studies in the Human Form*.

As he balanced on the wingback's uncertain springs, Dan gazed, disbelieving, at photograph after photograph of naked models.

Sitting. Standing. From the back. From the front.

Twice, Dan tried to stop, and, twice, he continued until, with a sliding sound, the clock chimed, and, startled, he returned the book to the shelf and the wingback to its usual position only to find that he was being watched.

"Fergus!"

Royal Crescent was a street in Irondequoit, a suburb of Rochester, New York, and Dan had once been at Sibley's, a department store in Rochester. He'd wandered off from his mother and had backed into a shelf of picture frames. One of them had fallen, and the glass had shattered on the floor, and a stranger, an old, toothless man, had grabbed his arm and shouted something angry. Frightened, Dan had pulled away and run to where his mother had finished in another section and was leaving, and he'd followed her, not telling her, not wanting to face her or the old man or any salespeople. Walking to the car, he'd kept looking back, expecting someone to come after them, and, on the way home, he'd kept looking for the flashing lights of a police car. For days, he'd expected someone to call on the phone or to appear at the door, which they hadn't, but that day, after looking at Mrs. Olney's book, he looked over at the Olneys' house so often that his mother asked him why. When he said he didn't know, she asked him what he was doing the rest of the day, and, when he said he didn't know that either, she said that she did, he was going outside, he and Tom, to do something, anything. She called Mrs. Petraglia, to see if her boys were home, which they were, so he and Tom went down the street to play football in the snow with Chris and Ricky Petraglia. It started as touch and quickly became tackle with the tackling getting harder and wilder until the boys were throwing themselves at each other, crashing, falling, and crashing again until Dan didn't think about the Olneys except to think, several times, that the Petraglias were more fun. They didn't play tennis, and they didn't ski, and they never said anything clever or funny. They were nobodies at school, and Mr. and Mrs. Petraglia were nobodies on Royal Crescent because Mr. Petraglia worked in a factory and Mrs. Petraglia worked as a secretary, but after, when he and Tom went, cold and wet, to the Petraglias' house, Dan thought that he should play with Chris and Ricky more often. He said yes when they asked him and Tom to stay for dinner and, after, to stay and watch television, after which their mother called and told them to come home.

"But there's no school," Dan protested before feeling as if Ricky had, as he had several times that afternoon, hit him in the stomach.

The cats.

He thought of Smoke and Fergus, sitting on the kitchen step, mystified by the still-darkened house. He thought of them giving up and wandering off, thinking they'd been abandoned, and he thought of something else. By the time he got home and went over, the street would be deserted. All the houses would be dark. "Fergus!" he called when he'd walked up the snowy tracks and opened the door and run through the house, turning on the lights until he'd turned on the back light and Smoke had appeared on the back porch but Fergus hadn't.

"Fergus! Come on, boy! Fergus!"

He flipped the back light on and off and called again and then opened the door and stood on the porch and banged a can of cat food with a spoon. When that didn't work, he went in and opened the can and gave the contents to Smoke and then walked through the house on the slim chance that he'd somehow left Fergus inside that morning.

"Fergus!" he called as he looked in the living room, beneath the couch and the wingback and the other furniture, no longer concerned about the books he'd looked at or whether he'd in any way changed their appearance.

"Fergus!" he called as he looked in the dining room and the den and the master bedroom, ignoring the other, larger, more detailed nude that was there and the nude sketches on the wall.

He looked in the bedrooms upstairs and all the closets, and he looked in the basement, now unafraid of what he might find in the dark. What could be worse than him? And what could be worse than losing the Olneys' beloved Fergus?

"Fergus!" he called. "Fergus! Fergus!"

Still consumed by the awfulness of what had happened and what he'd done, indirectly, to make it happen, he went outside and walked, calling, around the house and the house next door, the Kennards', and the house on the other side, the Greens', and then he went back to the Olneys' house and locked the back door and turned all the lights off and locked the front door and went home and told his parents. They told him not to worry, that Fergus would be back, that he'd be fine in the cold and would be waiting in the morning and, if he wasn't, he and Tom could make signs and put them up around the neighborhood and, if that didn't work, he could call people or walk around and knock on people's doors. He'll turn up, they said, but Dan knew he wouldn't. Each morning, he went over and fed Smoke and let her out and stayed for hours, checking the door and sometimes calling and sometimes walking around the neighborhood and calling. He'd go back in the afternoon and again, before dinner, and, once, he and his father went over. It was after dinner, and they sat in the living room, waiting, his father sitting in the wingback, right beside one of Mrs. Olney's nudes and right below the book with the pictures, a fact that Dan did his best to ignore.

"I lost a cat, once," his father said. "A stray, he just appeared one day—Mel, we called him. He used to sleep in my father's briefcase. We'd find him all over the place, but his favorite place was that briefcase when my dad came home from work and left it open on the kitchen table. And then, one day, Mel was gone, just like he'd arrived. We'd had him forever, it seemed, and then, one day, we let him out, and he never came back. So it isn't your fault, son. It isn't anybody's fault. It's just the way it is with cats."

His father was as bad as Reverend Vandertyne and his talks to the church youth group. "I know how hard it is to be a youngster," he'd say before starting some story that proved that he didn't.

His father was as bad as Aunt Ruth, who, that Christmas, had sent Dan a book about gem collecting. Who cared about gems?

"Dear Aunt Ruth," he'd already written back. "Thanks for the book. It's great. I hope your New Year's is great. "

Then, one morning, he started over and saw that the Olneys had come home. They'd returned the night before, and their car was sitting in the driveway, so Dan and his mother waited until they saw some lights, and then he watched from the kitchen window as his mother walked up the drive to the Olneys' front door and rang the bell and the door opened and she went in and, a minute later, the door opened again and she came out on the step with Mrs. Olney who had no coat and stood with her arms crossed and her head to one side. From the way Mrs. Olney leaned her head (the same way his mother leaned her head) Dan could tell that Mrs. Olney was upset but not angry except once or twice, for a few seconds, when she leaned her head the other way, opposite from his mother's. For the rest of the five or so minutes they were out there, their heads were leaning the same and nodding the same, his mother talking and Mrs. Olney's head nodding and then Mrs. Olney talking and his mother's head nodding, and then they both went inside and Dan looked at the house and wondered what they were saying until the door opened but this time it was just his mother who came out. She held the door with one hand and waved inside with the other, and then she closed the door and walked back down the driveway and back down the road with Dan still watching, still wondering what she'd said.

And then she came back in the kitchen, her hands and face white from the cold. "I told them the cat ran away," she said. "The rest is for you to know."

Summer Friend

After twenty-three years at the information desk, Rose could read people faster than any nurse or doctor in the hospital. Someone would walk across the lobby and say, "Excuse me," and Rose would know, from their posture or facial expression or tone of voice, whether they were going to see their dying father or newly delivered daughter or to tolerate another mammogram. "Can you tell me where Nancy King is?" a worried man asked, and Rose knew it was the oncology floor before she saw the woman's name on the printout that came from admitting every morning. "Can you tell me where Billy Hughes is?" a kid asked, and Rose knew from his sneer and the hour of the morning that Billy was in the Emergency Room, still getting stitched or casted after a night of no good. "Can you tell me if George Creahan is out of surgery?" How could she know before she looked at her sheets and then, not finding him, at her computer, that, yes, Mr. Creahan was out of surgery but had no room assignment, not even a bed number in recovery, a sure sign that he'd died on the operating table? Was it something that the questioners knew, some fear or hope that they communicated without knowing that they were doing so? How could she know more about people than they knew about themselves?

Never mind, after twenty-three years she did. Or thought she did.

So she was surprised by the pair that approached her one day after lunch. She'd eaten in the cafeteria and, despite herself, had eaten a slice of lemon meringue pie. She'd decided that she would and then that she wouldn't. She was in the cashier's line when, finally, it got the best of her. She hurried back and got a piece, and, feeling terrible but unable to return the pie or to bring herself to throw it away, she hurried through her lunch and the pie and returned to her desk, helping people on their way to one destiny or another as she planned to avoid, in the next month, the five hundred extra calories she'd consumed so inexplicably. She was deciding between salad without dressing and coffee without cream when the women appeared, two of them, both older although only one, the taller one, had hair that was altogether gray.

"Excuse me," she said, "could you help us?"

"That depends," Rose replied, unsure if she was being spoken up to or down to but sensing that it mattered. "Are you looking for a patient?"

"Yes."

"Can you tell me the patient's name?"

"Yes, of course—I'm sorry."

The first woman turned to the other as if it were her job to actually say the name, and, in the instant it took for her to do so, Rose noticed how trim the women were and how elegantly they carried themselves. Think of who we could be if we just stood up straight, her mother used to tell her, and, reflexively, she straightened, but it only made her feel the extra pounds she carried, one eighth of one of which was from her humiliating loss of self-control at lunch.

"Rita," the other woman said. "Rita McAlister."

Rose looked down at her sheets, flipping through them until she found the Ms and then the Macs and the Mcs, but there was no Rita McAlister. "I've got a MacKay, a McBride, a McTeague. I've got a McAlister, but it isn't Rita."

"Are you sure?"

"As sure as I can be."

"Then where is she?"

"I don't know. And she's not on my computer. Did she just come in? If she just came in, she won't be on my sheets until tomorrow."

"Her husband said she's been here all week."

"Then maybe she went home. Or maybe you've got the wrong hospital."

After Rose said that, there was no longer any doubt. The women were looking down at her. The shorter one looked peeved, and the taller one looked sad, as if Rose and the rest of the incompetent world were something to be regretted.

Then the taller one smiled. Faintly. Horribly.

"Barnes," she said.

"Excuse me?"

"Try Barnes McAlister," she said, and the other, shorter, woman looked ill.

"Here it is," Rose said when she found it. "Bigelow 10, Room 26."

And what do you think? Rather than taking the information and moving on, so Rose could tend to the next people, they stood there and considered it, as if wondering if it was right and, if so, if it was fair, and whether, as if there were any choice, they'd accept it.

"Bigelow *ten*," Rose said again. "Follow the blue line to the elevators," she added, anticipating their next question.

When, at last, they responded, she had the impression of the taller woman as a great but slow moving ship and the other as an escort, a tough little tug that helped her more powerful but less maneuverable friend with the finer points of harboring and setting off. The taller woman seemed to start her engines and slowly come about, and the shorter woman took her arm, and the two of them started down the line some earlier direction giver had decided the hospital should paint on the floor along with a red line and a yellow and a green, each branching off toward one or another of the hospital's many buildings. The General, as people called it. The Massachusetts General Hospital. You couldn't do any better. Whatever happened to you there would happen anywhere, Rose thought as she watched the pair walk from her desk back to where the lines began and led down the great central hall.

"Can I help you?" she asked the next person, a man looking for another man.

"Name?" she asked when the man nodded.

"Lopez-Malinowski."

"Full name?"

"Arthur. Arthur Lopez-Malinowski."

"Cardiac Care Unit. Follow the red line to the green line and take the elevators in the back."

Had Rose asked, the tall woman would have identified herself as Alice Link, of the New York Links, one of the great families of early America, which meant that she was related to several other great American families. Her 'great-greats' had been great when the great could only associate with their fellow greats (and date and marry them), so Alice was related not only to the St. Louis Links but to the Pittsburg Fallons and the Schenectady Johnsons and the vacuum cleaner Hoovers and, by marriage, the aluminum foil Reynolds. She'd been trained by a life of going to fine schools and listening to fine music and conversation and looking at fine art in fine cities to look at the rest of the world as she looked now at the signs in the hospital, as something that could, with a little thought, have been done so much better. Following colors on the floor. What were they, children? Laboratory animals? And what was a S.I.C.U.? a M.I.C.U.? a P.I.C.U.? Didn't anyone speak English anymore? Why was everything an abbreviation nowadays, as if no one had the time for words? And who was Bigelow? No one she'd ever heard of.

"Is this where we go?" she asked her friend at each turn in the blue.

"Yes," said her friend.

"This is it . . ."

"Now this . . ."

"O.K., here we go. Over here . . ."

Her friend was Lou, short for Louise, Louise Screery of the Nowhere Screerys, as she said when Alice needed a little putting in her place. They'd been friends since their days at Twin Rivers, short for the Twin Rivers Angling Association, a place their families had taken them once World War II was over and people had enough gas to take vacations again. Alice's family had a camp at Twin Rivers because they were rich and had whatever they felt like having, but Lou's family had a camp because her father was a doctor and made enough to have the things about which he really cared. One of them was fly-fishing, and he trained his children to land a fly on a rolled-up newspaper on the lawn of their suburban Hartford house before buying each a rod of his or her own and was careful to be, if anything, a little tougher on Lou than on Carl and John, her oldest and second-oldest brothers. The final test was fishing when the real sportsmen (and sports-ladies, he was careful to specify) fished, in May and September, a time when the salmon and trout were up from the bottom of the lake and in the rivers that ran into it. Maine was cold at those times and in the northwest mountains especially cold, and the children, if they came, were expected to take what pleasure there was in getting up early and waiting in the mist and the cold until, after a heart-pounding, barely believed minute of feeling and then landing a living, thrashing, brilliantly flashing fish, the impaled creature was admired in terse, if heartfelt, superlatives and released.

"Nice job, Lou," Dr. Screery would say, if that much. "A little brown, is it? a brookie? a salmon?"

There were twenty camps in all, cabins really, each owned by one family or one part of one family, some of whose other parts owned other camps, and, by chance, the Link camp and the Screery camp were next to one another. Before they owned it, the Screerys' camp was the Burkes', a family the Links had known as they'd known all the families at the association, by the condition of their camp and the number and condition of their boats and their cars and what little was said during chance meetings on the dirt road that connected the camps or what was said at the association's annual meeting. The fact was that the Links barely knew anything about the Burkes yet felt abandoned when Mr. Burke died and his wife got too old to come up on her own and their children were living too far away to stay interested. For several summers, the camp sat empty and Mr. and Mrs. Link tsked about the porch that was sagging, the paint that was peeling, the moss growing on the roof, and the accumulating broken windows until the cabin's sale was announced, and, the next summer, there they were, the Screerys, the father a doctor people said, the mother a former nurse, and the children, yes, everyone could see that there were children, three of them, two boys and a girl, although no one could say what they were like. As it happened, the boys and Alice's brother Peter were close enough in age that they were soon playing ball on the field by the caretaker's house and Alice and Lou were close enough to watch each other from one another's porch or dock until one day Mrs. Screery took Lou and walked over with a plate of freshly made cookies.

"Hi, I'm Jill," she said. "And this is my daughter Lou."

"I'm Madeline," Mrs. Link replied, kindly, although she was, of course, appalled.

It wasn't done at Twin Rivers. With the cabins fifty feet apart such overtures might lead to who knew what unwanted company? But in the awkwardness that followed, the girls had time to exchange a nervous glance. It was the first expression of a shared curiosity although, at that point, neither knew what question was being asked or when or how it might be answered. For her part, Alice sensed in Lou some respite from the unrelenting confidence and self-absorption of her father and brother and, to a lesser degree, her mother and the girls at her school. Just as she'd learned to appreciate fine things, she'd learned to appreciate fine feelings and to expect, eventually, to have a friendship based on such feelings. Even at ten, their age at that meeting, she could sense that Lou was at once more vulnerable yet stronger than other girls, less assured but more aware and more genuine, more present in a way that made her feel, almost at once, less lonely. For her part, Lou sensed in Alice a girl who didn't care, a girl (in those prefeminist times) who didn't care the way boys didn't care, the way boys were not only allowed but taught not to care, and she found it exciting. As the Link family's values were built on privilege, so the Screery family's values were built on competence, but male competence—on Dr. Screery's ability to formulate and give orders and Mrs. Screery's ability to follow them and to relay them to her children—and Lou was fascinated by this girl who either wouldn't or couldn't listen.

"Why don't I make tea?" Mrs. Link said in a manner that even Lou could tell was more dismissal than invitation.

"Are you in school?" she continued when they were all sitting down.

"Yes, ma'am."

"Do you like school?"

"Yes, ma'am"

"Ma'am, oh dear. Call me Mrs. Link. We're very relaxed here."

Mrs. Link poured the tea and then offered what she called "the fixings" and then the cookies to Mrs. Screery and then Lou and then Alice before taking a cookie for herself and pronouncing it delicious.

"Thank you," said Mrs. Screery.

But Alice said she didn't like hers.

"Alice!"

"I'm sorry, mom. I think it's the cinnamon."

"There isn't any," said Mrs. Screery.

"Then maybe it's the raisins."

"But you like raisins," said her mother.

"Then maybe I'm wrong," Alice suggested before shrugging and taking another.

Alice was spoiled, Lou was sure. But there was something that made it different, some childish simplicity, some life-affirming exuberance that made Lou want to protect it and to protect her. So the next day, when she saw Alice pacing around her cabin's front porch, she walked over and asked what she was doing.

"I'm running away."

"What?"

"I'm a poor slave girl. I have to work all day in the kitchen cooking food for my masters and carrying wood for the stove and then, when I'm done with all that, I have to clean their house and make all the beds and clean all the bathrooms and wash all the windows and do all the laundry, all of it for no money." She kept walking as she spoke, walking as if tired and holding her arms as if carrying a great burden on her back. She made another circuit of the porch and, without further comment, opened the screen door and went inside, and Lou followed her to her bedroom where she set down her imaginary bundle and said that she was home. "Do you want to be my long-lost sister?"

"Sure," said Lou.

"You can be my long-lost mother if you want."

"I'd rather be your sister."

"What name do you want to have?"

"I don't know."

"How about Lucinda?"

"O.K."

"Lucinda, my dear sister, look, it's me, Phoebe. I'm home at last. Now you say, Oh, Phoebe, I'm so glad you escaped from that terrible place. Welcome home."

"Welcome home," Lou said dutifully.

It had been ages since she'd had a friend unselfconscious enough to play the kinds of made-up games she still secretly enjoyed. Her mother found them tiresome and increasingly worrisome and her brothers found them laughable. Her father found them adorable, which was worse, so, for the most part, Lou either didn't play them or played them in her head. Suddenly, she had a friend who could see that nothing was what it was or that it was but only when it had to be. Suddenly, the association and all its cabins and the old horse barn and the old dining hall and the caretaker's house and the surrounding woods became places of unending magic and adventure. Some days Alice and Lou were sisters. Some days they were cousins. Some days they were runaway slaves or performers in a circus or detectives walking around the camp looking for the perpetrators of an imaginary crime. And some days they did things that Alice, too, had long wanted but thought impossible. Twin Rivers was on the shore of a lake with the unlikely name of Mooselookmeguntic. Some of the cabins were on the lake and some were on the Kennebago River, the camp being situated to take advantage of the fishing in that river and the adjacent Rangeley River. Unlike the Rangeley, the Kennebago was deep enough to canoe, and Alice had tried with Peter, but they'd argued the whole time, each telling the other how to paddle when, actually, neither of them knew. She'd said it didn't matter but had felt what she'd so often felt, that Peter was right, that everyone was right, everyone who said that she was clumsy and big and stupid and stubborn and was never going to be any good at doing anything until, one day, she tried it with Lou and was amazed at how easy it was. They paddled around the lake, in the water just in front of their cabins with their mothers watching and then, when they were a little better, out farther on the lake and then, the next summer, up the river on their own, and, the summer after that, they sailed around the lake in the Screerys' little sailboat. In Lou, Alice found someone with whom she could be a team, someone who thought her useful and helpful if only to take the orders Lou could never give at home. Lou never pounced on her the way her brother did. She never got embarrassed the way her mother and father did. She never took it personally if she told you to do something and found you staring off at a cloud thinking about something or somebody else. Whatever happened, she never looked as if you had, once again, kept her from some excellence her life, to that point, had led her to expect.

_____

And then there was Barnes, or Barney, the cause of their trip to the General.

Barney was the son of Arlene McAlister, the only tenured woman in the art history department at Yale, and Jim McAlister, a poet and perpetual adjunct with a list of glittering if temporary appointments at colleges throughout New England and the upper East Coast. Because Arlene worked when most women didn't and Jim worked not with tax codes or profit margins but with feelings and neither of them fished, they were considered peculiar as was their one and only child, a boy who, at age ten, not only spoke French but spoke it when you asked him a question he didn't feel like answering. How's it going, Barney? you'd say and he might tell you or he might turn and explode like a put-upon Gaul. And there were his naps in the afternoon and the stuffed animals he still slept with, and sometimes you'd find him in a tree, just up there by himself, for hours sometimes. And he didn't play ball. Or ride a bike. Or swim. Or have any friends. "He isn't a kid who makes friends," Arlene said as if, according to the latest thinking, it no longer mattered. Barney was, in everyone's opinion, a mess, if an interesting mess, and he was always of interest to the girls. He was, in grade school, the boy genius, the one who could name the American presidents and vice presidents and most of their secretaries of state and, in order, all the kings and queens of England. In high school, he could sing Beatles songs backwards, literally saying the words one after the other in reverse, and in college (too smart to stick with anything for long) he was forever reinventing himself, forever declaring himself premed or pre-law or pre-nothing, pre-Life he said, a poet like his father or an artist like the people studied by his mother, and for a while he threatened to go underground, whatever that was and for whatever reason anyone might want to. After a solitary childhood he led a frantically social adolescence, drinking and drugging and forever appearing with some "thing" as Alice and Lou called his nameless and largely speechless female attachments. And as the Sixties became the Seventies, as the world seemed to grow up with them, Alice had sex with Eliot, the boy she'd go on to marry, and Lou (unsuccessful at having a relationship of any type, sexual or otherwise) took a degree in social work and went on to head a child welfare department in Bridgeport, and Barney graduated from Harvard with no skills beyond what was needed to be a bright but unfocused undergraduate. Unable to find other work, he taught at a school in Vermont—for a year, he said. But that year became three, and then he met and married Rita, who taught French at the school, and then he moved from teaching English and sometimes history and sometimes geography to running the school, first running the English department and then the admissions department and, after several years, becoming assistant head. Eventually, he was back at Twin Rivers as were Alice and Lou, Alice with Eliot and their children and Lou with her parents or with her brothers and their children and Barney with Rita and their children. Eventually, they were the old-timers, the lifelong members who watched the comings and goings of the other old-timers and studied their cabins and boats and cars and, when meeting, promised sociabilities that didn't happen.

Only the past made them different, their shared past.

It meant that Lou could stay with her family sometimes but with Alice's family at other times and that, as Alice's children aged, they could come up, just the two of them, or meet in Bridge-port, or in Boston, where Alice lived with Eliot, or they could go to New York for the weekend or Montreal or, on one occasion, take a trip to France. And while Barney was, in some ways, excluded from their friendship, there were other ways in which they were and would always be close.

There was, for example, the time the Millikin boy and his college friends swam naked, in broad daylight, in front of the cabins. It was against the association's rules, but so was unpleasantness, so nothing was said until that year's meeting where Barney as president said, after the other business, that there was one more item to discuss. It had come to his attention that certain "not-to-be-named individuals" had been skinny-dipping and that they'd have to show more restraint. "Whoever you are, you've been spotted," he said, and Alice and Lou were amused by the number of private confessions his indirectness elicited, skinny-dipping being a long if private tradition at Twin Rivers and one Barney had enjoyed. Come on! his call had echoed through the starlit summer blackness. Chickens! he'd called to them and the other nervous but excited teens until they'd undressed and swum out and joined him and tried to talk of something other than their lack of clothes. Once, it was just the three of them, and they'd swum out beyond where they could touch until, suddenly, Lou was touching again. No, she was touching a something, she said, something big but something that moved, something that floated, and Barney swam over and said it was a snag, a tree that had fallen in the lake and been shifted about by storms and winter ice and posed a hazard to motor boats and swimmers unlucky enough to hit one when diving head first. He stood on it and then dared them to and then laughed as they stood, victorious and laughing themselves, while the black, starlit waves covered and uncovered their breasts.

And there was the time the Davis boy complained about the sewage system. It was old and out of code, and had been for years, and Twin Rivers, for all its affluence, had never gone to the trouble of replacing it. One year, the Davis boy came to the meeting and said that rich people were so sure that their shit didn't stink they thought they could dump it in other people's water, an opinion that Barney put to a vote.

"Stinkers say 'aye.' Or should they say 'nay'?"

"Oh, Barney," said Alice. "Really!"

Everyone knew what she meant.

Among the other personae he'd donned and doffed, Barney had been, for a few summers, an environmentalist upset about not only the sewage system but the boat motors that leaked oil and gasoline and the insect repellants that contained D.E.E.T. and the dues that were so high no one joined who wasn't rich and certainly no one who was black. He'd said that the place had once been the Indians' and should be returned. He'd been more critical than the Davis boy, by a long shot, and, with a word, Alice reminded him and everyone else, and a one-time assessment for the building of a new leach-field passed unanimously.

And there were other, more private, connections between the three.

One year Alice opened her mail to find a poem that Barney had written. It was so awful that she'd thought it the oeuvre of one or another of his children and that he'd sent it as he sometimes included, with his Christmas cards, Xeroxed collages of pictures they'd drawn or humorous recollections of things they'd either done or said. She'd thought it a parental excess, typical of so much about Barney that was in either over- or undersupply and about which nothing could be done. Only slowly did it occur to her that the mangled meter and unpredictable, sometimes-laughable rhyme could possibly be his and that he or anyone would have so little judgment as to do anything but throw it away.

> In the dusk, there's the musk,
> Of all that is and ever shall be
> Beyond us . . .

It went on like that for a page. What was she to do? In the end she did what she so often did, both with Barney and with the world generally and pretended it hadn't happened. She didn't reply and, when she saw him the next summer, didn't mention it, and neither did he, and it became just another of the awkward facts people of long acquaintance have to step around.

Then there was the time Trevor, his oldest, got himself arrested. Like his father, Trevor had been peculiar as a kid and troubled as a teen, and he'd done the same kind of experimenting with sex and drugs. Unfortunately, he did one of his experiments where a policeman could see it, and Barney called Lou because of her experience in such matters. Was she familiar with the law in Vermont? Could they send him away? Should he hire a good lawyer? He was sixteen and a half—would it go on his record? He discussed the case with a detachment more appropriate to a caseworker than a father, and Lou found their roles uncomfortably reversed. While Barney talked about blips on a screen and grades on a curve and this or that effect on Trevor's college applications, she talked about Trevor as a person, as a boy who was suffering in the there and then regardless of what might happen in the future. She said it as gently as she could, but Barney got mad and stopped calling, and the next summer, when she asked, he said that everything was fine.

"Oh, yes—that," he said, affably. "Thanks again."

And then there were the things they didn't share, things Alice and Lou shared with Barney but didn't share with each other and rarely admitted to themselves.

When Barney was at Harvard, Alice was at Barnard, and there'd been, at one point, a correspondence. Barney, as always, was floundering but, for a brief time, seemed to know it and to want to fix it and turned to Alice for advice. He called her about the camp, her family's camp, about using it one weekend, and she asked him who he'd be using it with, and he said it would be him and some girl he didn't care about and some friends he didn't care about either, and she asked why he was doing it. Did he care about himself? she asked, and he said no, he didn't, and then he started crying. "Oh, Alice," he said. "I love you, Alice. Did you know that?" Alice knew only that he'd probably been drinking and that the confessions that followed would probably be forgotten in the morning. Most of them were, but he called the next day and said never mind about the camp, he was going to find some new friends and maybe even a new girlfriend, and then he asked, laughing, if she was by any chance available. "Oh, Barney," she said. "*Really!*" But she responded when he sent her a letter. It contained a poem by Rilke, and she responded with one by Neruda, and he responded with one by Sylvia Plath. She wrote about the connectedness of things, about the links that people formed that were, given time, beyond time, and beyond any particular categorization of friend or boyfriend. She'd just met Eliot and was wondering if they should go all the way, as her classmates so unimaginatively put it. Who could think that with so simple an act, once, one had gone anywhere much less all the way? All the way to where, exactly? Who could think that Deborah Marchand, the tramp down the hall, had lived whereas Thomas Aquinas, Bernard Shaw, Beethoven, and Jane Austen and any number of other famous celibates had somehow missed out? In letter after letter, Alice expressed her suspicion that the Age of Aquarius was much like every other age, an age for men, an age in which men had freed themselves to have, in addition to whatever careers they wanted, whatever sex they wanted and had left women to cope with contraception and pregnancy and what the resulting children did to a woman's career. Alice was, in the letters, writing to Barney but arguing with Eliot, she was working out on paper her reasons for and against sleeping with Eliot, and, when she finally decided that she would and under what conditions, she said so in a letter and Barney nearly lost his mind. "To my surprise, I'm quite enjoying it," she wrote, and Barney was unprepared for the jealousy that seized him, for the scenes that he imagined. Never finding Alice more than adequately attractive, he suddenly saw her as beautiful, as smart and loving and, of course, rich, and in the arms of some sweet-talking punk who'd had every break a guy could have. In response, he called Lou and said that he was coming to her college, Middlebury. He said that he was coming up for Winter Weekend, that he had a friend who went to Middlebury (which he did) and that his friend had invited him (which he hadn't) and that ("if he found the time") he might come over to Lou's and say hello. He did so the minute he arrived, and Lou knew that something was wrong. Barney was drunk and, as the day progressed, got more drunk, and she knew, when he asked to stay in her room, that it wasn't because his friend was hosting his girlfriend that night and had no room for Barney. She knew that Barney was hoping, for whatever crazy reason, not only to stay in her room but to sleep in her bed, and she almost agreed. Unlike Alice, she thought that sex would change a lot. She thought it would give her that confidence, that silent but unmistakable sense of possibility that other girls seemed to have and that boys seemed to notice and respond to and that had nothing to do with good looks or good grades or good times or good anything as far as she could tell. She wanted, one way or another, to do it, to have it done as one might have something medical done—one's wisdom teeth removed, or one's appendix or gall bladder—and she thought that Barney would be as qualified to perform the procedure as anyone. It would complicate their summers, but they'd always been complicated, and at least he wouldn't rape her. At least she wouldn't have to see him every day and hear him walking around shooting his mouth off like all the other boys at Middlebury.

But just as they started, he paused. "Don't mention this to Alice," he said.

"What's this got to do with her?"

"Nothing. Forget it."

"No, tell me," she said. But he wouldn't.

"Oh God, I've been a bastard, Lou. About this. About everything."

He got up and got dressed and spent the night on the couch and left the next morning and never came back and never mentioned it again. Neither did Lou, and she never mentioned it to Alice, and Alice never mentioned the correspondence that had caused it. When the correspondence stopped, Alice realized that Barney had been writing with more feeling than he'd admitted and that she'd been guilty of the same. At some level she loved Barney, she realized. And what was even more unsettling, she loved him in ways that she would never love Eliot. In one of their exchanges, Barney had shared an anecdote about Neruda. He said that when asked what one thing he would save if his house caught on fire, Neruda had answered, "the fire." Many years later, she and Eliot were at the cabin enjoying a fire in the cabin's enormous fireplace and she remembered and told him. "Hmm?" he'd replied. "Oh, right. The fire. Passion. I get it." Eliot was a man like her father and brother, a good man, a strong if somewhat loud and insensitive man. Like Barney, he had many interests, including poetry, in fact, but his interests never seemed to consume and endanger him. They never seemed to cause what Barney mentioned in another of his letters, the kind of suffering that brings people closer to their souls. When Eliot went fishing, whether with Alice or by himself, it was to take a break from his big Boston law practice or the concerns of parenthood or the concerns of any man wending his way through a corrupt and complicated world. When Eliot went fishing, he either caught some or didn't but there was no concern that he would somehow get caught. When Barney fished, people wondered, would he capsize his boat and drown? Would he catch a hook in his eye and be blinded? Would he blind someone else? Would he borrow a pair of ill-fitting waders and slip on a rock in the Kennebago and break his neck? For Alice, Barney was like the teacups she was always spotting in antique shops and feeling the need to rescue simply because they looked so breakable or, even better, were already broken. Never mind that she already had a couple of dozen. Never mind that, every time she bought another one, Eliot told her she was crazy. "I know," she'd reply. But she didn't. She couldn't. It was a feeling she got from the cups, one she didn't understand but couldn't live without, just as she couldn't live without Barney and his various chips and cracks and missing parts. Alice loved Barney as she loved something breakable inside herself, whereas Lou loved Barney as she loved something inside herself that she also wanted, desperately, to break. Like her father, both her brothers had become doctors, and, for many years, Lou had hoped to do the same. In high school, she'd volunteered at a nursing home and, every Thanksgiving, at a soup kitchen, and, at Middlebury, she'd studied Spanish thinking it would be of use with migrant workers or the inner-city poor or medical work in Central or South America. She saw herself as the doctor her father was but better, as the doctor he should have been, working for those who couldn't pay, for those with lives so distracted and overwhelming they couldn't even thank her properly. She saw herself as the doctor her mother might have been had she been born in another generation. But she did poorly in biology and even worse in chemistry and was left, senior year, with only her good intentions and her Spanish. Having looked down at the girls who'd spent their high school and college years studying boys and how to catch and keep them, she found herself unable to do even that and unwilling to do what her mother had done, to become a nurse and spend a lifetime taking the orders she already so resented. She talked her father into paying for two years of social work school and talked herself into liking it and into liking the work that it led to, helping but also hating the dysfunctional families of Bridgeport, 'the worst of the worst,' she said with a distance she could never manage when talking about her own family.

What if she had slept with Barney that night?

Nothing! she told herself. But she could never quite drop it.

"Have you heard from Barney?" she'd ask Alice when they were together and such thoughts came to her, whether recognized or not.

"Oh yes, he called about a month ago."

Or he hadn't.

Or he'd sent a card. Or he hadn't sent a card. "Come to think of it, he hasn't sent one in some time," one or the other of them might say.

Whichever way it was, Alice and Lou would discuss Barney and what they either knew or didn't know about the latest in his life with a sense of ritual, even sacrament, with words that said what they felt and would always feel but also kept them from discussing what they couldn't. And they'd eventually discuss Rita. How emotional she was. How petty and materialistic.

"And what about—her?"

"Barney didn't say this Christmas, but the card he sent last Christmas said she was doing pretty well."

"That's good."

"Yes, it's something, I suppose."

Rather than criticize her directly, they discussed the cabin she and Barney bought and redecorated to look like a suburban ranch house with a full kitchen and two baths and wall-to-wall carpeting in the bedrooms and pictures of setting suns and pointing spaniels and leaping fish in the living room. Oh well, I suppose it's what she knows, they'd say. I suppose she thinks it's very nice, they'd say until one or the other of them noticed what they were doing and felt uncomfortable and talked instead about her illness, a lifelong affliction with which they more reliably sympathized. Shortly after marrying, Rita had a miscarriage, and then another and another until it was obvious to everyone but her that she had a problem. After each, she carried on as if there were no possibility of the next, each time announcing the pregnancy and her hopes for a boy or a girl and potential names and then, when each was lost, her grief and surprise. Lupus, Barney explained after she'd gone to the General for an evaluation. *Lupo*, the wolf: the disease was named for a rash that appeared on the patient's face, but Alice and Lou thought more about what was happening to Rita's body. It seemed appropriate that so inflamed a person should have an inflammatory disease. Barney said it was an over-reaction of the body's immune system, that rather than being aimed at something outside her body it was aimed at something inside, that her body was literally at war with itself and that, without medication, her kidneys and her brain and, eventually, all of her would be consumed. With the help of medication, she'd gone on to have children, two, Trevor and Becca, and thereafter her illness was only sometimes apparent. One summer, Barney and the children were up, briefly, without her. "It's her kidneys," he said, and nothing more. One summer, she came up but rarely left their cabin. "It's her joints," he said. "She has trouble walking." One summer she came up and acted strangely. She seemed to be drunk as Barney so often was, by turns seductive and attacking, pouty and gregarious, and was sometimes seen talking to herself. At one annual meeting she interrupted a presentation on the budget to say that Barney was having an affair.

"Go ahead!" she shrieked at him. "Tell them! You think I'm trouble! You think I'm a burden! You wish you hadn't married me!"

"Doing a little better here," Barney said that Christmas in his card.

He never used Rita's appointments as an excuse for the three of them or, if Lou came up from Connecticut, the four of them to get together. At the most, he'd say something after the fact, in a card or in passing the next summer.

"Back to see the bloodsuckers in Boston this fall." Or, "More tests at the General."

So Alice was surprised when he called.

"I'm 'n Bos—don," he said, his voice flat, his words badly slurred. "Ad duh General. And Ri—dah, she's here. Id wouldn . . . be fun . . . widoud Ri—dah."

"He sounded just awful," Alice told Lou after. "Absolutely potted, worse than I've ever heard him."

"Rita must be in a very bad way."

"Very bad."

"Poor Barney."

"Yes."

"And poor Rita."

"Yes. Of course. How awful for her."

Alice asked if Barney was, for the first time, asking for a visit, and they decided that he was.

"But how will I explain you?" Alice asked.

"I was coming up anyway."

"To do what?"

"To do anything. To hear the symphony. To see a show at the museum."

They decided that Lou was coming up so, after visiting Rita and Barney, they could continue up to Twin Rivers for the weekend. It had been a while since they'd been up there alone, they could say. If Barney wanted them to stay, they could stay, but if he didn't, or if Rita didn't, it gave them a discreet reason to leave. Look at the time, they could say as if they hadn't been watching it all along. We want to beat the traffic. We want to get there before dark. We want to get up in the morning and go fishing. "O.K.," said Alice, with the same resignation that the receptionist on Bigelow 10 said it when they arrived.

"Maryanne?" she asked the intercom on the desk in front of her. "Have you got McAlister today?"

"Yeah. Why?"

"He's got people here."

"How many?"

"Two."

"That's all?"

"That's all I can see."

"O.K."

"O.K.?"

"O.K.," said the nurse, and, once again, Lou and Alice started off.

But how could it be Barney, not Rita, at the General? And why had he sounded drunk on the phone? Was it medication? Was it some sort of tube in his mouth? Leaving the lobby, Alice had said simply, "Heavens!" and, waiting for an elevator, Lou had shaken her head and said, "What next?" Walking now from the nurses' desk to Barney's room, there seemed little point in saying more as they would, in a moment, know.

And so they did.

"Barney's had a stroke," Rita said when they found him.

He was lying in the nearer of two beds. He looked bloodless and small, and half of him didn't move.

"Wooo . . ." he said, visibly struggling with the name. "Ah—wiss . . ."

"He had a coronary bypass last week," Rita continued. "It's a known complication."

"But why did he have it here?" asked Lou. "Why not in Vermont?"

"Because his doctors are here."

"*His* doctors?" asked Alice. "But I thought—"

"You thought we came to Boston to see *my* doctors. We still do from time to time, but I've been in remission for years. Since Barney had his heart attack, we've been coming here for him."

"His heart attack?" said Lou.

Rita's voice was pleasant when she replied. "Didn't he tell you? I thought he told you ladies everything."

"Wooo . . ." said Barney. "Ah—wiss . . . tankoo fuh com—ing . . ."

Rita had risen from the only chair in that side of the room. She went to Barney and took his hand and left Lou and Alice to decide which, if either, of them should sit. It seemed wrong to keep standing but wrong to sit when Rita was standing, so Lou looked at the man in the other bed and, when he nodded, got the two chairs next to his bed and brought them over and sat down and waited for the others to sit down, which Alice did but Rita didn't.

"It was seven years ago. He was playing tennis in the heat. We brought him in to the hospital in Burlington, and that's what it was, a small one. When he was better we brought him down here to see what to do next, and they said nothing, just medicine and tests every year. But this year his tests were worse."

"You poor things!" said Alice.

"Yes," said Lou. But she felt—what? Not the concern she should be feeling, or not that alone.

It was the third summer of their friendship. They'd gone to Student's Island, the Links in their dory and the Screerys in theirs. It was one of the few times the two families did anything together, the wives being uncomfortable with each other and the husbands even more so. Whatever his abilities in the outside world, Dr. Screery was still an inferior in the world of Twin Rivers and had, therefore, to accept Harold Link's opinion on the suddenly darkened sky. "Nothing to worry about!" Harold said as the others nervously picnicked on. "Miles from here!" he said when lightning lit the clouds coming over Elephant Mountain. Then, with a single gust, the temperature dropped ten degrees, and they saw the wall of rain coming at them down the lake. They gathered their things and ran to the boats and clambered in, Alice and her brother and parents in their boat and Lou and her two brothers and parents in theirs, but by the time they were out in the wind-whipped waves it was clear that the storm was beating them. "Go to shore!" Dr. Screery shouted, this time not waiting for Mr. Link to agree. He turned the boat's little outboard and headed for a protected cove, and Mr. Link did the same, and, when they arrived, both families got out and hurried to pull the boats up and turn them over and crawl under them as the wind roared through the suddenly flimsy seeming trees and the rain pounded the old, wooden hulls and bolt after bolt of lightning exploded all around them. Lou and Alice crouched on all fours, squeezing together so that everyone could fit. They were so close that Lou could feel Alice trembling and, in the wildness of the moment, put her arm around her and held her. With each crash of lightning, Alice trembled and Lou tightened her grip, sending a series of long and intimate hugs that neither of them had the experience to understand. Had they been older, they might have seen that they were doing what women do when their men cause trouble. Had they been able to discuss it or to ask their mothers, the moment might have passed like any other moment of growing up. Instead it floated beneath the surface of their friendship like a snag floating beneath the surface of the lake, and when Lou ran into it—when some circumstance forced more proximity to Alice than she could tolerate—she rejected Alice as she did now.

"How are your kids?" she asked Rita, turning her back to Alice.

"They're upset, as you can imagine. Trevor's been here and gone, and Becca's coming tomorrow."

"How much longer will you be here?" asked Alice.

"Well, they're talking about a rehab facility. Another day or two here and another week or two there."

"And then?" Alice persisted, making Lou cringe.

How could she be so insensitive? How could she ask that with Barney there listening?

But Rita was unperturbed.

"The doctors say they don't know. They say he could be fine or he could have a few problems."

"Do they think he can go back to work?"

"Eventually," said Rita, and Lou was struck by how lovingly she looked at Barney and how lovingly he looked back.

For years they'd talked about Barney as if, with the right woman, he could have gotten so much farther in life. The unspoken conclusion was that the right woman was Lou, that she was more sensible than Rita, more practical and grounding, and would have helped Barney stay on task. With Lou, Barney might have been an academic like his mother or a poet like his father or a writer or a musician or almost anything. But as she looked at them now, Lou saw a truth pass between them, one they'd arrived at by the hard, honest work of living together, a work that she would never know. Maybe it had come from the loss of all those babies. Maybe it had come from living with the fear and uncertainty of Rita's illness. Maybe it had come from living with Barney's many failures and finding something more important than success. Whatever it was, Lou felt a sudden need to leave. She felt trapped by the sterility of the place, by its inhuman size, by the windows that wouldn't open, by the television the other patient was watching, by the harsh florescent light that seemed to counter any normal sense of day and night. She felt trapped by the food, by the sickening smell that was the same no matter what hospital you were in and what meal was being served, and by the faint smell of excrement and dirty sheets and by the chemicals used to clean them and by the busyness of the staff. And by Barney. Dear Barney. He was watching them from what seemed far away. He was watching them with one eye that looked like his and one that looked as if it belonged to someone else.

"I remember when my mother had her stroke," Alice continued. "She never recovered, of course, but she was older and had a lot of other problems. And you know, I was never all that happy with the nursing home we found her."

Nursing home! thought Lou. "They're looking for a rehabilitation hospital," she interjected. "That's an altogether different thing."

"I suppose," said Alice, "but the main thing is to find a good one. One where the people care, one where—well, where there aren't a lot of angry, underpaid immigrants who don't care about anything."

"Alice!"

"Well, it's true."

"Perhaps a truth that could be shared at another time."

"You're right. I'm sorry."

But she started again. About Barney's needs after rehab. About a home health aide. About equipment at home, wheel chairs and shower equipment and bidets. About insurance companies and how to get the most out of them.

Then she did what was, for Lou, even more unendurable. She turned to Barney and smiled. "I'm so sorry."

"Tankoo."

"You'll tell us if there's anything we can do?"

"I wuh."

"And Rita. You too."

"Thank you. Thanks to both of you."

There was nothing more to say. Or everything more to say. For a moment, it seemed that everyone might cry and, to prevent this, Lou touched Alice on the arm.

"I think we'd better be off," she said.

"Yes," replied Alice.

"Where are you going?" asked Rita.

"Twin Rivers," said Alice, and Barney convulsed. His head jumped from the pillow, and his face contorted, and he emitted a heartrending shriek something like that of a two-year-old child who's just fallen. "Hwaa!!" he screamed. "Hwaaa!! Hwaa!! Hwaa!! Hwaa!!" He was doing what many patients do in the first days after a stroke. He was exhibiting frontal release signs. He'd lost the pathways in the anterior brain that inhibit and modulate emotional expression, and he was screaming with the pain of a two-year-old, of a million two-year-olds, of all the millions of two-year-olds whose pains and pleasures had shaped the design of his and everyone's brains. Watching him, Lou was mortified. Alice was, at last, speechless. Even the man in the next bed struggled to sit up and see what had happened

Only Rita remained purposeful.

"It's all right, Barney," she said. "The doctors said to expect this. It doesn't change anything."

But Lou knew, as did Alice, that it had.

"Is this where we go?" Alice asked as they headed back to the elevator.

"Yes," said Lou.

"This is it . . ."

"Now this . . ."

"Here we go. Over here . . ."

And if few knew that Rose, at the information desk, watched those who walked into the General, even fewer knew that she watched, with equal attention, those who walked out. How else to know if she'd been right? The man she'd sent to find his wife in oncology, was he heartbroken? The boy she'd sent to the Emergency Room, was he smirking after seeing his good-for-nothing friend? The family she'd sent to find their dead father, were they bereft? Unknown to anyone, Rose remembered and watched for the people she'd helped, and she was watching for Lou and Alice when they reappeared. She'd imagined that they'd be in and out in a minute, that they'd pay their respects to some fellow hoity-toity and be off to something or someone more important. So she was surprised again, this time by how long they'd been and how worn they looked, how old and afraid. She was helping a man find his way to a surgery appointment, either in orthopedics or in sports medicine, the man wasn't sure and his card didn't say and the phones in both departments were busy. She was telling him to go to orthopedics and ask when she saw two women she didn't know and didn't know until they were almost back to her desk and then, to her surprise, she knew them exactly.

"Oh dear," she said so loudly that the next person, another man, asked what she meant. "Nothing," she said. "How can I help you?"

No longer worthy vessels pushing their way through an all too human sea, the women were flotsam, they seemed to bob and eddy toward the exit, which seemed only a temporary and precarious reprieve. As she told the man, a visiting doctor, where to find the auditorium, Rose watched the pair separate and go, single file, through the hospital's revolving doors and give a ticket to the valet outside. A moment later, as she told a woman where to find her colonoscopy, their car appeared, an old B.M.W. station wagon, Rose noticed, and Lou got in the driver's side, and Alice got in the passenger's side, and the car started for the exit, stopping at the place everybody stopped. At one place the road switched from two-way to one-way against you and you had to make a choice, you had to stop and turn left, back toward the city, or right, out toward the highway, and, as Rose inspected a man's bag, she saw the ancient car back up and awkwardly make a right, and then it was gone and she felt a small but definite loss. She didn't know these women or what had ended in their lives but felt, somehow, that it had and that it was deserving of her attention. She felt as if, wherever they were going, they wouldn't enjoy it, that they'd never again enjoy anything, although, about that, she was wrong.

True, Lou and Alice drove in silence for most of the four-hour trip. True, as they drove, the brilliance of the summer day seemed to mock them, and each familiar turn in the road, each rest stop and road sign, seemed to tell them of a distance they couldn't close. But when they got to the cabin, it was evening and Alice said they should drive the boat out to see the sunset. If they did, by the time they came back and unpacked it would be time for bed, and they could talk in the morning.

"Without feeling rushed," she said.

"What the place is for," Lou agreed.

And after that it was their bodies that did everything. Lou got a life preserver for herself and one for Alice and a pair of seat cushions, and Alice got a pair of oars, and they walked down the dock to where the boat was tied and got in, Lou in the front and Alice in the back. Alice vented the gas can and primed the line and then the motor and set the choke and pulled the starter once and then again, and then the motor started, and Lou untied the rope and pushed the bow off the dock, after which she pulled the bumpers and Alice switched the engine to forward and steered them out across the preternaturally still water. With Lou watching for snags, they continued past the other camps to the open lake until, at the meeting of Mooselookmeguntic and Cupsuptic Lakes, it was just them and the mountains and the water and the sky and Alice switched the engine back to neutral and then switched it off.

"It should be just a minute," she said as they began to drift. "That cloud needs to move. The one above Elephant. Is that Elephant or Aziscohos? I've never straightened out which mountain is which up here."

"I love you," said Lou.

"What?"

"You heard me."

But Alice didn't answer. "Shh," she said. "Look."

And there it was. The sunset.

A fire that filled the sky. A fire that filled their souls. A fire that, one day, would burn the world clean.

The
Home
of the
Holy
Assumption

Adeline Perry had been at Assumption for so long that she was part of the place. We'd lift her from bed every morning. We'd dress her in whatever clothes had come back from the laundry. We'd put her in her wheelchair and roll her to the television room, and there she'd sit, day after day, her mouth open, her face twisted, her glasses reflecting the stupidity of the morning talk shows, the afternoon soaps, and the evening news. There'd be a baseball game. There'd be a special report about a plane crash or a hurricane, or the President would be speaking, and there'd be Adeline, hanging from her harness, watching it all with a frozen half-smile until, one night, she was gone.

"Mrs. Perry," said Marienetta, the aide on nights. "Mrs. Perry is no here."

"Did you check the television room?" I asked.

"She is no there."

"Did you check the dining room?"

"She is no there. Mrs. Perry is no anywhere," Marienetta insisted, which meant that she'd checked the laundry and the chapel and the exercise room because the residents who could walk often wandered and one of our jobs was to find them.

"Bernie, you haven't got an extra resident on the second floor, have you?"

"Who'd you lose?"

"Mrs. Perry."

"Adeline Perry? How'd you lose her?"

"I was hoping that you'd know."

"Sorry, darling. I haven't seen her, and nobody's gotten on or off the elevator since I started my shift."

"Then where can she be?"

"Did you check the television room?"

"Yes, Bernie."

"Did you check the dining room?"

The daughter's name was Marilyn. She had a husband, and she talked about children who had their own children, and there was another daughter, Andrea or maybe Angela, and I think there was a son.

But I couldn't call them. "Donna, this is Joanne. I'm sorry to call you at home."

"What happened?"

"We've lost Adeline Perry."

"She died?"

"She disappeared."

"Are we talking about a resident or an employee?"

"She's a resident, Donna. You know her. She had a stroke. She's paralyzed."

"Then where could she go?"

"That's why I'm calling."

"Did you check the television room?"

"Yes, Donna."

"Did you check the dining room?"

Donna said that she wanted to drive in and look for herself, not that she didn't trust us, she said. And just after midnight, there she was, dressed in uniform, although the rest of us only wore white pants and maybe white shoes if we bothered to wear uniforms at all. She came to the desk, and she asked to see Mrs. Perry's record, after which she studied it, page by page, as if to find an error that would explain the disappearance. She asked to see the order book and the vitals book and the behavior log, and then she turned to Marienetta.

"When did you last see her?"

"Ten o'clock."

"Where was she?"

"Watching television."

"Was she alone?"

"I no remember."

"Did she look unusual?"

"I no understand."

"Did she look funny?"

"She look like she always look."

Donna grilled Marienetta, then she grilled me, then she went upstairs and tried to grill Bernie. He told me about it later. He told her that someone had called and asked for $50,000 or Mrs. Perry and her wheelchair would never be seen again. And she'd believed him. I could tell by how angry she was when she returned.

"Should we notify the doctor on call?" I asked.

"I don't think there's much he can do."

"Should we notify Sister Elizabeth?"

"She'll say we should notify the doctor. Do you know who it is?"

"Dr. Rasmussen."

"Is he good?"

"Good at what?"

"At this sort of thing."

As it turned out, Dr. Rasmussen had switched his call with Dr. Kendrick at the last minute, and Donna told him what had happened. He described a similar situation from several years earlier. A family had come to take a resident home on pass. They'd neglected to inform the nurses when they left, and the staff had been frantic.

"The Perrys can't take Adeline," I said. "She's a two-person assist with transfers. And Marienetta saw her at ten. Why would they take her in the middle of the night? Why wouldn't they ask to take her medicines?"

Donna made me place the call, and I hoped the phone would keep ringing.

"Hello?" someone said.

"Hello, this is Joanne Camerano. I'm a nurse at Holy Assumption. Is this Marilyn Stoshak?"

"Yes."

"The daughter of Adeline Perry?"

"Yes. Is there an emergency?"

"Well, I'm not sure, Mrs. Stoshak. That's why my supervisor asked me to call. She wants me to ask if you know where your mother is."

"My mother? She's at the nursing home. She's . . . who did you say this was?"

"This is Joanne, Mrs. Stoshak. We've met. I'm the nurse on the first floor."

"But where's my mother?"

"We don't know. That's why I'm calling. You didn't bring her home today did you?"

"How could I do that?"

"And no one else brought her home?"

"My sister lives in San Diego. And you can call my brother, but I can't imagine he would do it. And if he did, wouldn't you people know?"

I made Donna call Mrs. Perry's son. She dialed the number and sat, her spine straight and slightly away from the chair. She smiled and said hello and asked her questions, and when she finished, she set the phone down and stared at it for what seemed like a long time.

"It's time to call Sister Elizabeth," she said.

She made the call from her office, and I went to the nurses' desk to start my charting, and, right on schedule, Mrs. Kowalski appeared.

"Honey, could I have some grape juice?"

"Mrs. Kowalski," I said. "You know, perfectly well, that we don't have grape juice. We have apple juice, cranberry juice, and orange juice. We can give you one of those, and then we can help you back into bed."

"I want grape juice."

"Mrs. Kowalski . . . "

"Why can't I have what I want?"

"Mrs. Kowalski . . . "

"I am not a child."

I was still talking to Mrs. Kowalski when Marienetta said that Mr. Osborne had disconnected his stomach tube. She said his feeding had soaked his bed and made the floor slippery, so I should be careful in his room, which I was.

But Mrs. Kowalski followed me. I didn't see her in the darkness until I heard a scream and the kind of crack you hear when somebody fractures their hip by falling on linoleum. "I want grape juice," she said as Marienetta and Denise, the other aide on nights, helped me push a sheet beneath her and lift her to a stretcher. We rolled her to the desk, and I called Dr. Kendrick and Mrs. Kowalski's family, and as I was holding for the triage nurse in the Emergency Room, Donna returned.

She looked like one of the residents. "Sister Elizabeth wants to fire me."

"What?"

"She said that I've been promoted beyond my training."

"Get outta Dodge!"

"She said that I've compromised the future of Assumption."

The Home of the Holy Assumption—or the Home of a Number of Assumptions as Bernie called it—was operated by the Little Sisters of the Poor, and every year they talked about closing us. The home was too small to be efficient, they said, or it was too big to be efficient, or it was too dependent on welfare cases or not dependent enough. The Little Sisters were always discussing the future of Assumption, and Sister Elizabeth was always discussing the ways that we'd compromised it. You don't care enough. You don't work enough. You use too many paper towels.

"Sister Elizabeth says that to everybody," I said, but Donna disagreed.

"Not to me," she replied. "Not like she said it tonight."

The triage nurse picked up, and I told her what had happened as well as Mrs. Kowalski's allergies, medications, and medical problems.

"At least *she's* taken care of," I thought before discovering that the night's activity had woken the other residents as well. Mr. Thomas reported a stomachache. Mrs. Cleary felt feverish. Mr. Donovan convinced Mr. Winshall that the building was on fire, and Denise said that Mr. Piva was having chest pain.

"He do it again," said Marienetta, shaking her head as she passed me and Mr. Piva. "Mr. Osborne. He pull out his stomach tube. He do it again."

Mr. Mercier worked in the kitchen. He didn't say much, and I never knew if his English was poor or he was angry or just quiet. "All right . . . ," he'd say if we greeted him. "All right . . . ," he'd say if we asked about the meal trays.

But that morning, when he arrived, there were Donna and Sister Elizabeth. There were the residents, up and wandering. There were the police, and there was Mrs. Perry's daughter and son, and there was what looked like a reporter.

And there was Mrs. Perry.

There were two elevators, and unless there was enough traffic for the call button to activate the second, it sat, its doors closed from the departure of the evening shift until the day shift arrived the next morning.

"Mother of Jesus!" Mr. Mercier exclaimed when the second elevator opened to reveal Assumption's first successful escapee.

"He say he kidding," said Marienetta. "But he scared. I scared. Everybody scared."

A wandering resident had found Mrs. Perry and rolled her onto the second elevator just before it had gone quiet for the night. The resident, unaware of what he or she had done and unable to report it when asked, had gotten off before the doors had closed, and Mrs. Perry, unable to call out or to press the buttons, had sat, imprisoned for eight hours, but none the worse for the experience as far as we could tell. We checked her blood pressure. We listened to her lungs. We cleaned her up and changed her, and, after we fed her breakfast, we rolled her to the television room. What else could we do?

"Live and learn," said Donna. "We'll have to make a new policy for the elevator."

"Good for Mrs. Perry," said Bernie. "I thought she had some fun left in her."

"The Little Sisters will never understand," said Sister Elizabeth. "This event has compromised the future of Assumption."

I had the next day off. And the day after that I didn't start until eleven, and Mrs. Perry was in bed. I didn't see her until the following day.

"Hey, Adeline," I said when I got to the television room. "It's me, Joanne. Hey, you know what I heard? I heard you tried to leave without paying your bill."

But the woman didn't move. She didn't blink. She sat, hanging from her harness, her frozen face smiling as if she hadn't missed a thing.